SRCH

CAERPHILLY COUNTY BOROUGH COUNCIL

3 80

D1492660

RIS

16 MAR 2013   -5 JAN 2018

18 SEP 2013   -9 OCT 2018

26 MAR 2017

22 APR 2016   Tynnwyd o'r stoc
30/6/16   Withdrawn

24 AUG 2017
27 Nov 17

CAERPHILLY
COUNTY BOROUGH COUNCIL
CYNGOR BWRDEISTREF SIROL
CAERFFILI

Risca Library
01443 864780

Please return / renew this item by the last date shown above
Dychwelwch / Adnewyddwch erbyn y dyddiad olaf y nodir yma

BITTER BLUE

Manchester private eye Sal Kilkenny has a new client – elegant hotel receptionist Lucy Barker has been receiving offensive poison pen letters, and the strain is starting to show. Meanwhile, Mr and Mrs Ecclestone ask Sal to get some background information to help their house purchase. As she prepares to stake out the streets a bitter cold snap brings arctic conditions. On the home front, why is Sal's daughter Maddy reluctant to go to school? As her surveillance duties bring a grim discovery, her other problems escalate … and there is one more nightmarish surprise for her.

BITTER BLUE

BITTER BLUE

by

Cath Staincliffe

Magna Large Print Books
Long Preston, North Yorkshire,
BD23 4ND, England.

British Library Cataloguing in Publication Data.

Staincliffe, Cath
    Bitter blue.

    A catalogue record of this book is
    available from the British Library

    ISBN   0-7505-2086-8

First published in Great Britain 2003 by
Allison & Busby Limited

Copyright © 2003 by Cath Staincliffe

Cover illustration by arrangement with The Old Tin Dog

The right of Cath Staincliffe to be identified as the author of this
work has been asserted by her in accordance with the
Copyright, Designs and Patents Act, 1988

Published in Large Print 2004 by arrangement with
Allison & Busby Ltd.

All Rights reserved. No part of this publication may be
reproduced, stored in a retrieval system, or transmitted in any
form or by any means, electronic, mechanical, photocopying,
recording or otherwise without the prior permission of the
Copyright owner.

Magna Large Print is an imprint of Library Magna Books Ltd.

Printed and bound in Great Britain by
T.J. (International) Ltd., Cornwall, PL28 8RW

This is a work of fiction and all characters, firms, organisations and instants portrayed are imaginary. They are not meant to resemble any counterparts in the real world; in the unlikely event that any similarity does exist it is an unintended coincidence.

Thanks again to Maggie, Mary, Jane and Julia.

For Tim: the adventure continues ...

Chapter One

I ran like mad to reach my office: legs
aching, lungs bursting, cheeks aflame, my
bag banging against my hip. Hoping that my
new client would still be there, that she'd
hang on when no one answered the door at
the Dobson's house. That she'd been delayed
too.

Why today? School re-opening after the
Easter holidays and Maddie, my seven-year-
old, had mutinied. She'd refused breakfast
saying she had tummy ache. When I told her
that a lot of people felt the same the first day
back she began to cry. I sent Tom to get
dressed and tried to find out why Maddie
suddenly thought school was the worst
place in the whole world. Was it the work,
her teacher; had something happened? She
wouldn't elaborate.

'We'll have to go, love. Go brush your
teeth. We'll think of something nice to do
later, something to look forward to?'

She shot me a filthy look.

'I can write Miss Dent a note; tell her

you're a bit upset.'

'No,' she blurted out, horrified at the idea.

'Maddie, you need to go in. You'll be fine once you get there.'

'You don't know...'

I glanced at the clock. Late. 'So tell me?'

She shook her head, gave a sob and turned to leave the room. I moved to hug her and she pushed me away.

She also refused to hold my hand on the walk there. Six-year-old Tom ran ahead, stopping to kick anything unattached and practising scissor jumps. When we got to the school gates there were a couple of other stragglers but the place had that deserted look. Everyone in registration. I handed them both their lunch boxes, gym kits and book bags. Tom gave a wave and ran through.

'Do you want me to come in with you?' Hoping she'd say no.

She shook her head.

'You'll be okay,' I reassured her.

'Can you see I've been crying?' She rubbed at her face.

'No.' It was true the red eyes and streaked cheeks had vanished though she didn't look happy.

'We could invite Katy for tea,' I said. Katy

was her best friend; she'd joined the class at the beginning of the year.

She shrugged. I resisted the temptation to sigh. I kissed her head. 'Off you go.'

As soon as she was out of sight I turned and pelted along the pavement. Arriving late and flustered was not how I wanted to present myself to a new client. I really needed the business. I turned into the side road and slowed to a quick march. It wasn't raining yet, though more was forecast, and it wasn't all that cold. Please let her be there. Please, please.

I wonder now how long she would have given me? Another five minutes? Ten? If I'd walked instead of run, if Tom had forgotten his lunch box or Maddie begged me to chaperone her, if it had been raining, if I'd slipped and broken my ankle ... if, if, if. Then maybe none of it would have happened like it did. None of the whole, stupid, bloody mess of it.

As I neared the house I could see her, back to the door, scanning the street. I gave a wave and turned into the drive.

'Miss Barker?' I said as I reached her.

A slight inclination of the head.

'Sal Kilkenny. I'm so sorry, I got delayed.

15

Have you been here long?'

'Quarter of an hour.' Her tone was cool, her lips a thin, red line.

But she'd stayed, she hadn't given up and gone home in a huff. I could soothe the waters, win her round.

I unlocked the door, my breath still laboured, hands trembling a little from the run but immensely relieved.

My office is situated in the basement of the Dobson's family home, near where I live. They don't need it and so for a modest sum I have dedicated space away from home which, so the theory goes, I can lock up and walk away from when my working day is done.

I led my new client downstairs and into the room. It was cooler in there and I switched on the convector heater, hung up our coats and offered her a drink.

'Coffee would be nice.' Her manner softened a little. 'Just milk please.'

'I forgot to ask you on the phone, how did you hear about me?' It's useful to find out how clients arrive.

'Yellow Pages, you were the nearest to me.'

Word of mouth counted for the bulk of my enquiries, the rest came via the phone book as this one had.

'Where are you?'

'Levenshulme,' she smiled.

I guessed she was in her late twenties. She was slightly built with glossy brown hair which she had drawn back and clasped in a leather barrette. She wore small gold teardrop earrings and an engagement ring on her left hand. Her eyes were almond shaped, blue like faded denim, her mouth small, the lips coloured a high gloss carmine shade. She wore a tailored red suit and court shoes, that along with the polished make-up, made me think of an air-stewardess or a beautician. Someone whose job description included the words well-groomed. Elegant not flash.

I handed her coffee and sat down opposite her at my desk. As yet I'd no idea why she required the services of a private investigator. She had booked an appointment without disclosing her problem. A lot of people do that; they prefer to speak face to face.

Blowing on my coffee I took a cautious sip. Then pulled pen and paper towards me. 'What can I do for you?'

'It's this.' She opened the black leather handbag on her knee and drew out a sheet of paper. 'Came through my door.' It was folded in half. Plain paper, A4. She slid it

across to me. Nodded that I should open it.
I did.

YoU arE DEAd BITch

I flinched: an instinctive reaction. A death threat.

Four words. The letters taken from different sources, newsprint, magazines, stuck side by side.

I met her gaze.

She pulled a face, her shoulders joining in the shrug. 'I want you to find out who sent it.'

Looking back at the note it was clear that the sender had done all they could to preserve anonymity. No handwriting and not enough text to give any clues away. It hadn't been an impulsive gesture, a scrawl of pen, posted in the heat of the moment. No. Whoever had sent it had assembled newspapers, magazines, scissors and glue, they'd selected, cut and pasted, stewing in their hatred and then they'd gone to Lucy Barker's and delivered it. Two questions: who and why? The answer to one would lead to the other.

YoU arE DEAd BITch

Not whore or slag but bitch. Redolent of anger, of someone done wrong but perhaps not specifically of sexual jealousy. Bitch. You

18

are dead. With one intent: to frighten.

'When did you get it?'

'Last week. Wednesday, when I got in from work. Just there.'

'No envelope?'

'No.'

That meant no postmark, even less easy to trace.

'Have you any idea who might have sent it?'

'No. There was one before, exactly the same but it just said bitch. I threw it away.'

'How long ago?'

'About a week earlier.'

'Have you had any disputes with neighbours, problems at work, boyfriend trouble?'

'No.' She shook her head, the tiny earrings jiggled.

'Anything else odd – phone calls, feelings of being watched, anyone hanging around, acting suspicious? Anything at all?'

She stared at me, an element of surprise on her face. 'Yes. One day, I thought there was someone round the back of the flats, I just saw this movement. I thought perhaps someone was putting their rubbish out but no one came back in.'

'Have you reported this to the police?'

'I don't want to,' she said quickly.

'I think you should consider it. A threat like this.'

She held my gaze. Blinked. 'I want you to look into it.'

I took a breath. 'It will be very difficult for me to trace. If not impossible. They've made sure that there's nothing here to give them away. There are no clues,' I explained. 'No handwriting, no postmark. Nothing unless someone saw them posting it at your house. And I'm not equipped to check for finger-prints, anything like that.'

'Can't you do anything?'

Thinking for a moment, I stared at the note. 'If I took the case I'd approach it from the other end.'

She frowned.

'Rather than spend time looking at that,' I tapped the letter, 'I'd concentrate on investi-gating among your friends and acquaintances to establish if there's anyone with a grudge. Something like this, there's usually some history there. It comes down to finding the connection between you and this person. You'll see from the contract that I guarantee a set amount of time but I can't guarantee a result. It could be intrusive too. It would mean talking to people at work, to family and friends.'

She took that in, indicated that I should carry on.

I took her details. Her name was Lucy Loveday Barker. She gave a shrug explaining Loveday was an old family name. I'd guessed right about her age, she was twenty-nine. She worked as a receptionist at the Quay Mancunia Hotel in neighbouring Salford. Five star. Hence the grooming – or maybe she was that sort of woman anyway. She had a flat in a Victorian detached in Levenshulme near the Alma Park estate. Her parents had emigrated to Australia some years after her only brother went out there. She had trained in hotel management and worked in Leicester and before that in Kent.

When I pressed her on the issue of enemies she couldn't think of anyone who bore her ill-will.

'What about the past? Relationships gone sour, disputes at work, financial problems, old family feuds?'

She shook her head.

'And your friends, have you told them about this?'

She shook her head. 'I didn't like to,' she said quietly, 'I just wanted to forget about it, I suppose but ... I began to get a bit

21

frightened.' Her hands tightened on the bag. 'I rang you.'

'Your fiancé–'

'There's no one,' she interrupted.

'Just the ring, I thought...'

'Oh,' she gave a little gasp. 'No,' her cheeks flushed. 'I was engaged, that is...' Her eyes filled.

'I'm sorry,' I felt clumsy at my mistake. But why wear a ring that misleads?

'Benjamin died,' her voice faltered.

I murmured more apologies but she shook her head and carried on. 'It was a long time ago. Sudden. A car crash. I don't always wear the ring but sometimes I want to remember him. I'm sure it sounds stupid but it makes me feel closer to him.'

She took a drink, became calmer.

'The note was hand-delivered,' I said. 'Do you have separate letterboxes at the flats?'

'Yes, at the front door. There are five apartments and we have one each.'

'And that's where you found this?'

She nodded.

'It could be a case of mistaken identity. A grudge against one of the other residents?'

She frowned. I noticed her eyebrows, thin dark brown arcs, more pencil than hair. 'I hadn't thought of that. But our names are on letterboxes. And this is the second one.'

Yes. If you went to all this trouble, you'd make sure your nasty little message reached its target.

Drinking some coffee, I considered my response. I wanted the work but I don't do the hard sell. It's better all round if my clients hire me with their eyes wide open.

'As I see it, you've three choices.'

She swallowed, replaced her mug, gazed at me with total attention.

'You can do nothing, ignore the notes and hope they lose interest, perhaps come back if they persist.'

Her eyes told me exactly what she thought about that for starters.

'You can report it to the police and see what they suggest...'

A crisp shake of the head.

'...or you can hire me. If you do that I'll put my energy into trying to shed some light on who's behind it.'

'Yes. I want you to do that.'

'And if I can't come up with an answer?'

'I'd still feel reassured, I think. Like a sort of insurance.'

'Okay. We need to make a list of all the people in the different circles in your life and pull out a few who you really trust, people I can talk to.'

The names she came up with were other managers at the hotel. She explained that work had been demanding since her move to Manchester a year before and if she did socialise it tended to be with colleagues. As for her neighbours she knew them all in passing but no better.

'And there's not been any aggravation at home? No noise disturbance or quarrels about parking?'

'Nothing at all.'

We agreed that I would speak to her colleagues first, the ones she trusted completely, and enlist their help, but without revealing all the details of Lucy's problem. The neighbours would be next. In a perfect world they would have seen the note being delivered and have photographic recall of the person carrying it. Their description would fit a person named by the hotel as having a vendetta against Lucy. I'd confront them, threaten police and they would apologise and desist. Case solved. In a perfect world ... I'd be out of a job.

Lucy Barker opened her handbag. 'You said you'd need paying in advance. Is cash all right?'

I smiled. 'Cash is great.' And I felt my own

sweet sense of relief as I drew out a contract. Work equals money. I wouldn't have to increase my overdraft. Everything was going to work out fine. As Tina Turner sang to Ike. Before she turned and ran.

Chapter Two

It was most likely that Lucy Barker knew the person who'd sent the letter. Of course, if Lucy was a random victim, if the person's motives were illogical or bizarre I'd have next to no chance of detecting them.

Meanwhile I'd assume that the sender intended Lucy to get the mail as a result of some trouble between them. The upset may have seemed so insignificant to Lucy that she'd forgotten all about it but the poison pen writer had nursed their grievance and it had grown big enough to prompt a campaign of intimidation.

You hear stories of inappropriate reactions all the time. They get given catchy tags: road rage, air rage, trolley rage, parking rage. Accounts of people losing all control over tiny slights. Violence erupting at the traffic lights and the ticket office. Punching, stabbing, ramming, beating. Strangers going for each other's throats. But that sort of over-reaction was spontaneous, unforeseen. This was planned, measured.

One of the people on the list I'd got from Lucy might be able to recall some bad blood or ill-will that Lucy had overlooked. And there was always a chance that one of them might be the letter writer, even though Lucy trusted them. So when I spoke to them I'd be listening not only to what they said but also what they avoided, looking at their body language: the loud gestures of folded arms and tapping feet and the smaller but more specific signs from eye and lip movements. Using my intuition too, relying on gut feelings to pick up on the atmosphere; psychic sonar to detect hostility beneath the surface or anxiety lurking behind their replies.

As for the neighbours, there were four other flats at the Levenshulme house and most of the residents would be out at work during the day. Sitting back I stretched then consulted my diary. The next day, Tuesday, or Wednesday after tea would be a good time to call on them if my housemate, Ray, could look after the children then.

Lucy had asked me to be as discreet as possible when talking to her three colleagues at the hotel. 'I don't want the whole place to know,' she had said. 'It's awful for gossip. Could you talk to people after work or on their lunch hour?'

I rang Malcolm Whitlow, security manager at The Quay Mancunia Hotel, and told him I was carrying out a confidential enquiry on behalf of one of his colleagues. Was he free for lunch?

We arranged to meet in the Terrace Bar Cafe at The Lowry. I had a brief prick of worry about money until I remembered the cash. Lunch at the Lowry. I hadn't eaten out for ages. Okay, it wasn't going to be three courses and wine but it beat a cheese butty and brinjal pickle hands down.

The Lowry is in Salford, Manchester's neighbouring city. Walk down from Deansgate and you've crossed the border. Manchester is a poor place really. Behind the hype of city centre living, with flats going for a cool million, the glitter of Manchester United and the tacky glam of *Coronation Street*, there's a dull, deep seam of deprivation. Struggling schools, crumbling hospitals, early death rates. Top of the pops for all the really heavy

27

stuff like cancer and heart attacks and young male suicides.

Manchester and Salford share much of the same history of wretched poverty and vibrant struggles for social justice. The Chartists and the suffragettes were among their long line of radicals. Salford is the original dirty old town. With destitution and decline off the scale the city flogged off assets, mainly land, declared itself a Free Enterprise zone and secured funding to re-create itself as a vast urban theme park. Down came the slums around the deserted docklands and up went chi-chi gated communities and marina developments. An audacious Lottery bid brought money for the Lowry. I don't know what happened to all the people who used to live in the warren of terraces that had been swept away. But I don't think they moved into the smart new apartments.

I drove towards Salford Quays past the huge chain sculpture that stands with its links soaring upwards, defying gravity: a memorial to the docks, and within sight of the Old Trafford stadium, home to Manchester United's Red Devils. Heavy plant machinery were busy carving out yet more ground for the next big development.

The Lowry is a stunning steel and glass creation, reminiscent of a great ship when viewed from across the water, which has won accolades for its design and for its success as an attraction. I'd seen a couple of shows at the theatre there with my friend Diane. Ray and I had brought the kids to the galleries a few times. Nana Tello, Ray's mum, had come with us once but she complained that the curving walls, sloping floors and the bright orange and purple decor gave her vertigo. I liked it – the colours were like my office. The centre houses Lowry's paintings, depicting Salford at the height of the Industrial Revolution: smoking chimneys, blackened brick dwarfing the drab-coated, ant-like figures of the new working class. Here and there a three-legged dog, a child skipping, a moment's laughter.

After parking in the high rise I crossed the open, cobbled space to the arts centre building. The wind was picking up now, the clouds above were full and round like boulders, the colours of granite and slate.

The Terrace Bar Cafe is situated in the prow of the building with a vista out across the quay to the new Imperial War Museum North on the opposite bank. Curves and soaring geometric shapes clad in aluminium.

Another breath-taking design though I could never quite read it as a globe in shards as the architect, Daniel Libeskind, intended. Arriving a few minutes early, I ordered an orange juice and took a table. A break in the clouds admitted a wide beam of sun which glanced off the choppy water in a thousand quivering diamonds.

It was easy to spot Malcolm Whitlow when he arrived. He had the bulk and stance of an ex-policeman and a suit that screamed bouncer. He was probably only in his early forties but the lamb chop sideburns in iron-grey, receding hairline, a smoker's creased face and rasping voice all conspired to make him seem older.

Introductions done, we consulted the menu. Malcolm picked the sausage and mash with onion gravy and a pint of Boddingtons, our local beer. I chose a sundried tomato ciabatta and another juice. I ordered the food at the bar and joined him at the table.

'Thank you for seeing me. Not everyone likes dealing with a private investigator.'

He waved away my comments. 'Nah! I've a couple of mates in the same line. Checked you out.'

I cocked my head, mock bow. Wise man.

'You said one of our staff was having some bother?'

'That's right. I don't want to go into too many details at this stage.'

He raised his eyebrows; they were nicotine yellow.

'Are you aware of any tensions among staff?'

'Can't say I am. Though you'd be better asking personnel.' He took a swig of beer which left a drift of foam on his upper lip. 'Without a name...' He licked the foam away.

He had a point and his caution worked in his favour.

'Lucy Barker. I'm trying to find out if anyone has a grudge against her.'

He grunted, thought for a moment. Shrugged. 'Not that I know of.'

'Is she well liked?'

'Yeah. Well, she pulls her weight, turns up on time, she's pleasant enough. That's all that matters when you're working with someone.'

'Does she manage any other staff, as the receptionist?'

'The assistant on the desk, trainees. And she has quite a bit to do with other areas: housekeeping, the restaurant. If someone makes a complaint she'll handle it – front line sort of thing.'

'What about hiring and firing?'

'She'd be on the interview panel,' he agreed, 'and she'd do the probation report and the appraisals for her staff.' He hesitated, his eyes brightened. 'There was one girl...' He leant forward.

'Yes.'

'While back, two, three months. Hopeless slacker, never made an effort. Took the hump if she was told off.'

'Miss Barker sacked her?'

'No. Gave her a warning. But she was caught pilfering, complimentary flowers and bubbly. Instant dismissal.'

'You remember her name?'

'Jowett, Carly Jowett.'

'If she had a grudge who would it be against?'

'Me, I reckon,' he laughed.

We were interrupted by our food arriving. Once eating was underway I returned to my questions. I'd a hunch that Malcolm would be in acute need of a nicotine fix once he'd cleaned his plate and eager to get outside.

'Any other staff who might have resented Lucy Barker?'

'No,' he spiked his sausage, 'can't think of any.'

'Guests?'

'You always get one or two who like a moan but there's not been anything out of the ordinary.'

'What about personnel records, how would people get hold of them?' Thinking that someone had Lucy Barker's home address.

'It's all on computer, admin staff have the password. It's confidential.'

'And letters, application forms?'

He nodded as he chewed. 'Files. They're kept locked.'

'Have any other staff come to you recently with concerns, anything at all?'

He shook his head, took a swig of beer. 'Nope. Not a dickey bird.' He frowned. I could tell he was dying to know more but I still thought it was prudent to play my cards close to my chest.

'She all right?' he asked. 'Is it something serious?'

'Not pleasant. She wants to get to the bottom of it.'

He shuffled in his seat. 'If it affects the hotel – I'm responsible for security.'

'It happened at home.' I told him. 'Obviously if it had been at work you'd be the best person to look into it. If you hear

33

anything, notice anything, you'll get back to me? Or if you think of anything else?' I passed him my card.

'Yep.' He scooped up mash and gravy.

'I'd like to keep this quiet.'

He nodded his agreement.

I finished my sandwich and drained my glass. Malcolm polished off the last of his meal. We talked for a minute or two about the security world: how technical it was becoming, the impact of computers and electronics, the gadgets available. Then I thanked him for his time and left.

Carly Jowett, warned by Lucy then sacked by Malcolm Whitlow. What would Lucy say about her? Two months or more seemed like a long time to wait but then it's in the nature of grudges to grow with nursing.

Chapter Three

There was a message waiting for me on my voice-mail. A couple called Ecclestone were considering buying a house but had some concerns about the area and wanted to know more about the neighbours. I returned their call and arranged for them to come and see me the next day.

Walking down to school I had a prick of anxiety about Maddie but they'd have rung if she'd had any major trauma. I waited in the playground; the sky was a dismal grey, a quilt of cloud. I nodded to other parents I knew and watched a pair of toddlers shove at each other until one of them fell over and began to wail. Tom came out first of his class, his teacher with him.

'Are you Tom's mum?' She was fairly new and hadn't yet got to know everyone.

'No, I'm Sal. I live with Tom and his dad. My daughter Maddie is in Year Two.'

Her eyes had a glazed look. She dipped her head in a little gesture that suggested she wasn't going to try and follow all that. 'Well, he's had a bump.'

He had too. He brushed back the black curls from his forehead to show me a shiny egg-sized lump. 'It doesn't hurt,' he said.

The teacher gave me the standard concussion letter. We wouldn't need to worry. Tom bounces back from falls and tumbles like a kelly in a budgie cage.

We crossed to the other door where Maddie's class came out. She emerged, one of the last, on her own, trailing her gym kit

35

and looking glum.

'How's it been?'

She shrugged.

'Did you ask Katy for tea?'

She shook her head.

'Maybe another day, then?'

Another shrug.

'I could have a word with her Mum now?'

'Can't we just go home?' she snapped.

'Fine,' I sighed.

Tom chattered to me on the walk back while Maddie stayed silent. I knew from past experience that probing wouldn't help. She'd tell me when she was good and ready. Maybe there wasn't anything specific, she could be sickening for something (please no!). She was a fairly moody child, sensitive to slights and quick to lose confidence. I often wished she'd more of Tom's resilience.

The two of them were like brother and sister, or maybe step-brother and sister. They were growing up together. Tom's dad, Ray Costello, is a single parent like I am and we share the tenancy of the house. It's always been a platonic arrangement and we'd never blown it by falling into bed together on the rare occasions when one of us has had a sudden, foolish craving for intimacy.

That April, Ray was firmly ensconced with

girlfriend Laura, and I was single after a short-lived romance.

Digger the dog greeted us rapturously at home but only Tom paid him any attention. I left them rolling on the hall floor playing wolves and took the lunch boxes and book bags into the kitchen. Maddie went into the lounge and put the telly on. Maybe she just needed to chill out a bit.

I put potatoes in the oven to bake and began to tidy the kitchen. If Carly Jowett was the poison pen letter writer how had she got Lucy Barker's address? I put the plates down and went into the hall for the phone book, sat on the stairs and leafed through it. No listing. How easy would it be to sneak a look at personnel files? Or to find out where someone lived by listening to the chit-chat? Idle talk about districts and house prices, routes to work, landlords, could all have given clues.

When Ray got in at half past five we all sat down to eat together. Maddie picked at her food, rearranged it on her plate, but I didn't spot her actually swallow anything. Was she getting ill?

Ray looked incredibly smart. He had a charcoal wool suit on, crisp white shirt, his black hair and moustache trimmed. He's got Italian blood and when he dresses up he looks like something out of a De Niro movie. He'd been for a job interview with an IT company. He wanted regular work; furniture making is his real passion but never makes him much money.

'How'd it go?'

'Good. Yep. They'll let me know by the end of the week.' He grinned obviously pleased with his performance. 'Told them I wanted half-time, flexible if possible.' Ray was committed to his share of childcare. Over the years we'd worked out a system that suited all four of us.

'And?'

'Bit of throat-clearing, odd raised eyebrow but they've a whole new department to staff. And they were very specific about whether I'd be free to start in May.'

'A good sign. Hope you get it.' I passed round seconds of coleslaw and tzatziki. 'Tom banged his head.'

'Look.' Tom showed him.

'How did you do that?'

'Ran into the wall.' He gave a little sigh.

'Didn't you see it?' Ray joked.

'I had my eyes shut. I was a zombie.'

At this point Maddie would usually have cast doubt on Tom's intellect or rolled out the latest slang insult but she seemed detached from the conversation.

'Are you in tomorrow after school?' I asked Ray.

'Here all day,' Ray replied, 'I can take and collect, too.'

Great.

I rang Lucy Barker to warn her I'd be talking to her neighbours the following evening. I would call on her then as well; things had come up I needed to ask her about. And I wanted to visit the flats so I could see where she lived and picture someone delivering the letter.

I could fit the remaining two Quay Mancunia staff in on the same day if I planned it right: Pam Hertz, the housekeeping manager for lunch and the general manager of the hotel, a man called Ian Hoyle, after that during working hours. One visit to the hotel itself wouldn't alert anyone to my enquiry. I'd ring them all first thing. And if Maddie was ill Ray would be home to look after her. Sorted.

I was at the office with time to spare before house hunters Zoe and Frank Ecclestone arrived. Middle-aged, middle-class, they wore matching polar fleece jackets. His with cords and Timberland boots, hers with suede trousers, ankle boots and a paisley neckerchief. He was bald and had grown a large beard to compensate. She had carefully streaked blonde hair down to her shoulders. She wore an Alice band. I could imagine her on a horse.

I'd tidied up the place a bit. It doesn't take long; there's only a filing cabinet, a few shelves, chairs and my desk there. The dirty cups I washed upstairs in the Dobson's kitchen. I'd dusted the large blue painting that my friend Diane had done for me and straightened the blue rug that practically covers the floor.

The Ecclestones sat side by side opposite me and explained what they wanted.

'We love the house.' Zoe Ecclestone gave me a copy of the estate agent's leaflet. 'And the area's very definitely on the up...'

'Buoyant,' Frank added.

I glanced at the address; Severn Road, West Didsbury. One of the priciest parts of Manchester. Anything in Didsbury (East, West or the village) is highly sought after. The area is favoured by celebrities, media-types and property investors; it's only a few miles from the town centre and handy for the airport and motorways south of the city.

For many Mancunians, Didsbury is the posh end. But the Ecclestones were right to proceed with caution. Didsbury had its fair share of car thieves and drug dealers. In Manchester the other side of the tracks is never more than a stone's throw away.

'...but a lot of the properties have been divided into flats, some are student houses. If it's going to be parties every night...'

'...drunks in the street...'

'...then we'd rather keep looking.'

I studied the photo. The house, 'Chestnuts', was an impressive Edwardian semi which boasted lots of original features. Mature gardens, four bedrooms, master ensuite, cellars. The fashionable West Didsbury location had pushed the price up to a cool £289,000.

'Is it occupied at present?'

'No. The owner died. She was in her eighties.'

'And have you met any of the neighbours?'

'No,' she looked a little shamefaced.

'We thought you...' He left the sentence dangling.

'Of course.'

A peace of mind report. The phrase is most often used in the trade as a euphemism for spying on suspected adulterers. People either get peace of mind or their worst fears confirmed and the whole world blows up in their faces. However, for the Ecclestones, instead of lurking outside hotel bedrooms or eavesdropping on lunchtime liaisons, I'd be sizing up the street, establishing whether anyone nearby was running a brothel, dealing drugs, feuding noisily with the neighbours, breeding rottweilers, bashing cars about all night or re-creating the headiest Ibizan raves in their front room.

'What I suggest is that I carry out surveillance of the area at various times over the next week; particularly at night and the weekend when any noise is likely to be at its worst. I'll also talk to residents on either side of your house and opposite and provide you with a written report high-lighting any concerns. I can have that ready for you Monday morning. And that would be covered by the standard peace of mind fee.'

They exchanged a glance. 'Super,' she said.

She produced a fountain pen and wrote me a cheque in neat script, blowing on the paper to dry the ink. We agreed I'd fax the report to them. They could then ring me if they had any queries about it.

Once I'd seen them off I spent a little time catching up on routine administration and answering my e-mails. I was due to meet Pam Hertz, housekeeping manager, for lunch at 1.30 and after that to see Ian Hoyle, the Hotel Manager.

Setting off early meant I could visit Severn Road, where the Ecclestones hoped to move, on the way. It was raining lightly, Manchester drizzle; it muted the colours of red brick and the green of the mature sycamore and horse chestnut trees that canopied the road. I parked opposite the house 'Chestnuts' with its For Sale sign and studied it as well as the properties either side.

They were substantial three storey semi-detached with steeply pitched roofs, bay windows and fancy brickwork on the corners. Each top storey window was arched and had a small balcony. Stone gateposts still stood but the original railings and gates had long gone – probably melted down during the second world war and now replaced by privet hedging or walls. Chestnuts' other half, 'Oakview', on the right, looked as if it was still a family home. No row of bells, cheap tarmac parking bays or mismatched net curtains to suggest multiple occupancy The door had been freshly painted a racing green and the old sash windows looked in good repair. Conifers and shrubs in the front garden were well tended, the yellow forsythia and the lilac were in flower. And a Dicentra, the bleeding heart plant with its graceful foliage, was full of buds in a chimney pot planter by the front door.

The house to the left of Chestnuts told a different story. A concrete forecourt replaced any garden and a sign on the wall stated that the property was let and managed by Carver Estates. I made a note of their number. It looked to be a decent conversion, the windows were uPVC and the place seemed in good repair. It was impossible to tell whether it was let to students or professionals. Some places had leases that just ran for the academic year, and the constant turnover would make it hard to predict what the neighbours would be like to live with. If the flats were on long term lease and let to professionals then the population would be more stable and some would argue less disruptive. Whoever lived there, I would still need to find out if they were likely to cause any disturbances. Look behind the labels to the reality. There was no one about at that time of day and no cars parked out front. All out at work?

On my side of the road sat the properties opposite the Ecclestones'. The house on the left of the pair appeared to be business accommodation. There were two plaques beside the front door – though I couldn't make out the lettering – and vertical slatted blinds masked the large downstairs window. I got out to get a better look. Severn Insurance and Mannion & Shaw. I walked along to the gateway of the adjoining house. Desolate: a torn yellow curtain was pinned across the bay window and upstairs what looked like sheets had been stretched across the bedroom windows. A rusting car on blocks sat in the driveway and an overgrown garden boasted dock leaves and dandelions with torn carrier bags and crisp packets caught among brambles. An overflow pipe dripped steadily from the gable and along the edge of the roof the guttering sprouted grass and seedling sycamores. The place was an eyesore and would be visible to the Ecclestones every time they looked across the road. I was surprised that in itself hadn't put them off. Was it empty? Looked like it.

Driving up and down the length of the road it was clear that most places were being renovated and redeveloped for multiple-occupancy or had already been. To Let signs be-decked every other place. One huge detached pile had two skips in front of it, stuffed with rubble. A good time to be a builder, a plumber or plasterer.

At nearby Burton Road, the main street, there was a bohemian feel to the range of outlets: Thai, Korean and Indian restaurants, designer clothes outlets with titchy clothes at gigantic prices, handmade furniture and crafts places, kitsch gift shops. And alongside them the places found in every Manchester high street: hairdresser, sun salon, iron-monger, junk shop, mini market, video store and charity shop. All a little scruffy round the edges. Would it suit the Ecclestones? They seemed more upmarket, more Cheshire than Manchester, but I was making assumptions. She might design zinc pots, teach T'ai Chi and love browsing for bargains for all I knew. Or perhaps they'd zip off in their four wheel drive to shop out of town and ignore the uneven retail opportunities on their doorstep.

I took Princess Parkway, the big dual carriageway, into town and made my way again to the Lowry. This time my lunch guest joined me in a ciabatta and coffee.

Pam Hertz, in charge of housekeeping at the Quay Mancunia Hotel, had something of the schoolmistress about her; perhaps it came from the brisk, no nonsense replies to my questions, her habit of referring to her staff as 'the girls' and the clipped, slightly too-loud voice she used. She wore a suit in the same style as Lucy Barker's but she had plumped for navy. I'd been very cagey when I'd set up our meeting and she began by asking me briskly what on earth it was all about.

I explained I was working for a colleague who had been involved in an unpleasant incident. She tutted and snorted.

'How can I possibly help you if I don't know who we're talking about. Besides you might be up to no good, I'd need to know the person involved was happy for me to talk to you.'

I gritted my teeth, dialled Lucy's number at the hotel and asked her to give Pam Hertz the all-clear. Pam Hertz listened. I saw she was surprised that it was Lucy and nodded. She handed me back my phone.

'Poor girl.'

When I began my questions she mentioned Carly Jowett. 'A nasty piece of work.' But she couldn't recall any other feuds or fallings out between Lucy Barker and her work mates.

As we were concluding our meeting I sensed a moment's unease. Pam Hertz made to speak but hesitated. It was out of keeping with her general manner and I picked up on it.

'There's something else?'

'I don't for a minute think that this is relevant...'

'Go on please.'

'Really...' She began to dissemble.

I smiled to reassure her. 'It all helps me to get a rounded picture. And I don't go leaping to conclusions.'

She nodded. 'Nicky Prince, she was on reception with Lucy until recently, well ... Nicky asked for a move, to my department. She found Lucy a little ... intense. Nicky's getting married soon and Lucy, she lost her fiancé.'

'Yes.'

'Well, Lucy wanted to know all about Nicky's plans and apparently she'd keep comparing them to what hers had been, the flowers, the reception – everything. It made Nicky uncomfortable, that's all. As I say there's absolutely no question of it being any part of this...'

'No, I see. But it is helpful to know about.'

'Nicky's a sensible girl. And I don't think Lucy had any notion of what was behind the transfer. You won't say anything?'

'No.' My responsibility was foremost to my client but there was a degree of tact and diplomacy in deciding what I reported back. I operated on a need to know basis. But perhaps I should talk to Nicky Prince.

'Is Nicky working today?'

She shook her head. 'No, she's still on honeymoon. A fortnight in the Maldives.' We shared an envious glance. 'Not back till the weekend.'

Which effectively ruled her out as a suspect. She'd been basking in tropical bliss when Lucy's letter was delivered.

Before we left I asked Pam Hertz to be discreet about my enquiry too, Lucy knew I was meeting her but the rest of the hotel didn't need to.

'Of course. Will you be speaking to Ian Hoyle?'

'Yes, this afternoon.'

'He's the one with the overview and he runs personnel. He really ought to know there's something going on.'

'We don't know yet whether someone from the hotel is involved.'

'Oh, I see. All the same, if it involves Lucy then–'

I nodded. Thanked her for seeing me.

I freshened up in the Ladies before leaving the Lowry for the hotel. The drizzle blurred the light on the canal and swathed the buildings in a wreath of grey. It brought out the smell of wet concrete and the sewagey scent of river water. A forlorn ice cream van was parked beside the turning circle used by coach parties. People were heading for the arts centre in a steady stream but they ducked their heads against the soft mist and didn't linger to appreciate the architecture.

Chapter Four

Quay Mancunia, five minutes walk away, oozed modernist luxury. The main entrance of curved glass doors opened onto a circular foyer with white walls, a carpet like a painting, abstract shapes in earthy tones, and enormous pieces of rock and driftwood sculpture set around the place among drifts of pebbles. At the far side of the foyer was the reception area, lifts and doors through to the administration offices.

If Pam Hertz and Malcolm Whitlow had been appropriately guarded but personable and co-operative I found Ian Hoyle a prize pain in the neck. How he'd ever got the job of manager was beyond me as he exhibited none of the people skills which I thought were essential in modern management.

We got off to a bad start.

'I must say that I'm not exactly happy to find a member of staff has chosen to spend their money hiring a private detective when we already have an excellent in-house security team.'

'I've spoken to Malcolm Whitlow; he's fully aware of the situation.' And *he* didn't have a problem with it.

But Hoyle looked exasperated. His nostrils slightly flared and the edge of his lips were white with tension. He had moody good looks, a tall, slim frame and sported day-old designer stubble.

I explained to him as succinctly as I could mentioning Lucy by name and told him what information I wanted.

'What makes you think it's someone here?' He played with the hole punch on his desk, pushing it to and fro.

'It may not be. I'm trying to eliminate

people as well as identify anyone who might have a score to settle.'

'Can't think of anyone.'

'How easy would it be to get hold of staff addresses?'

'They're locked in there,' he nodded at the filing cabinets, 'the computer entries are password protected. You think whoever it is might try and find out where Lucy lives?'

Innocent or clever? Devious, I know – but twisted thought processes are a tool of the trade.

'Do people know each other's passwords?'

He reddened a little. Was that a yes?

'I'll change them.'

He looked at his watch. Stood abruptly and moved to open the door. 'I really must get on.'

My cheeks flushed with indignation. What was his problem? Had he sent the notes? Surely he'd want to keep his head down, deflect suspicion if he was behind it? So why the waspish attitude? The sudden end to the meeting?

I remained seated. 'How is your working relationship with Lucy Barker?'

He glared at me, a twitch rippled across his right cheekbone. 'Fine.' He made it sound like a curse.

He opened the door giving me no option but to leave. I was baffled at his manner and decided to be direct.

'Mr Hoyle, have I missed something? You seem to resent answering my questions but I'm only trying to protect one of your colleagues. You were one of three names she gave me – people she trusted? Is there something I need to know?'

He closed his eyes momentarily and sighed. He glanced at me and made an ineffective flapping movement with his arms. 'No, sorry.' He sounded exhausted now. 'Pressure, problems at home, nothing to do with this. Sorry.' But he made no move to resume our talk.

'If you think of anything else, will you get in touch?'

He nodded. Exhaled noisily. He ought to be off on sick leave if things were so bad.

'I'll leave my card.' I put it on his desk and gathered up my coat and bag, relieved to come away. When Lucy had given me his name she'd made no mention that he was going through a difficult patch but maybe he'd been hiding it from them all? And now the façade was cracking. Perhaps I'd been the first to witness it. How long before he started bawling out the staff, drinking from his desk drawer or letting his work slide? Lying about reports and hiding his in-tray in the filing cabinet? Whatever the trouble at home was he needed to deal with it or take time off to weather it.

Maddie seemed perkier at tea time. She talked a bit about their school topic and the Roman Temple they were making and she ate most of her spaghetti. She was on the brink of reading to herself but still enjoyed being read to. We spent a peaceful quarter of an hour on the couch, with Roddy Doyle's *The Giggler Treatment*.

Levenshulme, the neighbourhood where Lucy lived, sprawls either side of the A6 road to Stockport. Most of the area is terraced housing with tiny backyards. Home to a large Irish community and more recently a sizeable Asian one. Near the railway station and towards Burnage were bigger places, built for the professionals and the managers rather than the workers from the biscuit factory or the nearby mills. The big villas came substantially cheaper than equivalent properties in Didsbury. Levenshulme was not a fashionable area and there were many more signs of neglect, although Stockport Road itself had undergone a thorough facelift and a regeneration scheme was ongoing.

Lucy Barker's detached house was on a corner plot and there was enough land around it for residents' parking and some landscaped garden. The house had no immediate neighbours. There was a small park to one side and a disused chapel to the other with boards over its windows and padlocked doors. Five garish yellow burglar alarms clung to the house's brick walls – rather spoiling the Victorian period details. A border of shrubs softened the iron railings that ran around the perimeter and to either side of the front door steps were box trees trimmed to cone shapes. Once I got close I could see they were chained to bolts set low in the walls.

The building had cellars, and narrow basement windows ran just above ground level, protected by wrought iron bars. The ground floor was in fact several feet above the ground and broad stone steps led up to the blue front door.

I examined the letter boxes at the left. As Lucy had said they were each labelled with the number of the flat and the surname of the occupants. I tried the door, which was firmly locked. The intercom system at the right featured a row of bell pushes, again with names attached. I pressed Lucy's, identified myself when she answered and pushed the door when the buzzer sounded.

The lobby was pure Victorian; black and white floor tiles, dark green and sage walls, the lighter shade above the dado rails, a broad staircase straight ahead with a large stained glass window on the landing above featuring tulips.

Lucy opened the door to her flat. She still wore her scarlet suit though she'd taken off her shoes.

'You said you had some questions?' She looked a little anxious.

'Yes, a couple of things people have mentioned. I'll go over it when I've had a word with everyone else.' I pointed up the stairs.

Half an hour later I had spoken to Adam Chan, a teacher, who answered the door with a kitten clasped in his arms; Mr and Mrs Conroy, NHS staff, who spoke rapidly in such rich Belfast accents that I had to ask them to repeat things; and Maria Creasy, a violinist with the Halle orchestra who had gone mad with the citrus air freshener to try and mask the cannabis smell in her lounge. And all I'd got for my trouble was a whole heap of noes. No one was aware of any tensions between residents, no one had received threatening mail or abusive phone calls, no one had seen anything untoward, no suspicious visitors. I watched their reactions carefully and didn't detect any hint of subterfuge.

They all expressed some concern for their neighbour, though none of them knew her as anything more than a passing acquaintance. They promised to keep their eyes and ears open.

The students, R. Osunde and D. Abacha, were out and, given they'd only moved in a month or so previously, they weren't high on my list of people to talk to.

At Lucy's I accepted coffee and settled in an armchair. The room was a horrible mixture of styles: ragrolled walls in blue with stencilled borders and matching curtains were dated while the furniture, which I assumed to be Lucy's, was floral and fussy; cottage prints in green, pink and white which clashed with the blue. I was surprised, I'd expected her flat to mirror her dress sense; crisp lines, clear colours, objects artfully placed. Lucy didn't look as though she belonged there.

I told her about my fruitless trek round the

neighbours and she nodded, a trace of disappointment in her eyes.

'Tell me about Carly Jowett.'

'Carly?' She looked puzzled.

'The girl who was sacked for stealing.'

'Oh, that was ages ago ... must have been ... early February. Just before Valentine's Day. That's why I remember: Benjamin and I, we wanted to ... we were going to get married on Valentine's Day.' Thankfully she didn't get all upset again but I recognised the intensity that Pam Hertz had mentioned, the dwelling on her own lost marriage plans and the death of her fiancé which had discomfited her co-worker.

'You don't think Carly Jowett's behind this do you?' She was slightly incredulous.

'I don't know yet. Her name came up. Tell me about her.'

'Not a lot to tell really. She had no discipline. She came over well in the interview but she was late for her shifts, poorly turned out, not as helpful as she should be with the guests. I had to give her a formal warning; a verbal one.'

'How did she take it?'

She tilted her head to the side while she found the right word. 'Resentfully, sullen. Like a child.'

'And then?'

'It was the following week, Malcolm asked me to go to his office. Carly was there, she'd been caught stealing: champagne and flowers. She was dismissed.'

'And how did she react to that?'

'"You can stuff your effing job",' Lucy quoted. 'But I don't think she sent the letter.'

'Why not?'

She gave an impatient shake of her head. 'It just seems like an awful lot of an effort and a long time since. She was caught red-handed. It's not like she was treated unfairly. And it was Malcolm that caught her, not me.'

'Maybe she thought you'd tipped him off?'

She shrugged. Not convinced.

'What about Ian Hoyle?' The mean and moody manager who couldn't wait to see the back of me. 'How do you get on?'

Something flashed through her eyes. Surprise? Fear? Hard to tell because she recovered well. 'Fine. Why?'

'I found him a little ... brusque.'

'Oh,'

Oh? Was that the best she could do? There was an awkward pause. She was hiding something. I could smell it as the time stretched between us.

'He didn't seem very keen to help. I don't know why?'

She kept her mouth shut, her eyes on the mug in her hand.

I waited.

'He can be a bit off-hand,' she offered. 'It doesn't mean anything.'

I studied her. Flawless skin, glistening lips, a lie slithering through her eyes.

I took the risk of being rude. I'd been paid after all. 'If you're not straight with me it only makes my job more difficult.'

Anger snapped across her face then she put her cup down. 'It's silly, just a silly mess, that's all.' She looked up at me from under her lashes. 'I'm not Ian's favourite person at the moment. It wasn't ... I hoped it wouldn't matter, or I'd have told you. He ... he had a crush on me. They're expecting a baby, I think things are a bit tricky at home. It was silly. I told him not to be ridiculous. He knows it's for the best. Men!' She gave a brittle laugh. I didn't join her.

'Did anything happen?'

'A kiss, a meal. I offered a shoulder to cry on, he completely misread the situation.'

Had it gone further? She'd kept this from me, was there more?

'Why didn't you tell me?'

'I didn't think it was important.'

On what planet, exactly? Woman spurns man, woman receives anonymous letters, calling her a bitch, making death threats. My money wasn't on Carly Jowett anymore.

'Really,' she leant forward, her palms together, fingers pointing at me. 'It's not Ian. It's not his style. Besides, he's too much to lose.'

It was a feeble disclaimer in my book. People risked everything more often than we liked to imagine.

'He'd never do that.' Or she didn't want to accept he would.

'He's the most likely suspect from where I'm standing.'

'No,' she insisted.

'He is.'

'Let me talk to him.' She said. 'He's having an awful time at the moment. They're not sure whether the baby ... there may be something wrong. I'll talk to him.'

'I don't think that's a good idea. And he's not going to admit it, if it was him.'

She thought. The tips of her fingers pressed against her temples. 'I know it wasn't Ian. I'd swear on it. But if it was, and I really don't believe it, not in a million years, then it would have been a moment of madness and he'll be eaten up with regret. He'll tell me,' she nodded emphatically. 'He's mixed up at the moment but he's a decent man.'

'I'd rather speak to him again myself.'

'No,' she said stubbornly, a hard edge to her voice.

I took a breath. 'My professional opinion, the reason you hired me...'

She raised her palm to stop me. 'I'll speak to him tomorrow, I'll ring and tell you all about it. I don't want him harassed any-more.'

'Harassed?' Now she was really getting my goat.

'He's a friend.'

What could I do? Lock her in her flat? Dump the case?

'I'm not happy about it.'

Silence.

Stalemate.

She ran her thumb along the edge of her other nails. 'You've spoken to everyone on the list then?'

'There's still the students here.'

She shook her head dismissively, echoing my own sentiments.

'And Carly Jowett. I'd like to rule her out.

There won't be much more I can do after that. Unless I start to try and trace the lettering, but that will only give us the sources that were used and they are probably publications anyone can get at their local newsagents.'

'Maybe we'll never find out,' she said philosophically, 'you said that might be the case but at least we'll have tried.'

I still felt uneasy as she showed me out. Frames hung beside her door: pictures of a young man and a couple of Lucy.

'Benjamin?'

She nodded. Lowered her almond eyes. I couldn't think of anything to say that didn't sound trite.

Lucy opened the door.

'Be careful with Ian,' I said, 'if he's very stressed...'

'It'll be fine,' she said.

She stood on the steps and gave a little wave as I drove off, looking for all the world like an air-stewardess bidding farewell to a planeload of passengers.

Chapter Five

It was dark, just after eight o' clock, but I hadn't finished work. Time to put in my first stretch of surveillance on Severn Road, to see on behalf of the Ecclestones whether the area was a pleasant place to move to. I hate surveillance; it's tedious as hell unless someone's on the run and then it gets scary. However, as I charge double rates for it, when I get brassed off I just think of the money. Getting cold and wanting to pee are two of the technical problems. At The Four In Hand, a nearby pub, I made use of their toilet facilities. I'd already sorted out a packed supper to keep me going and even brought along an audio-book complete with a portable cassette. An old pro, me.

There was space to park near the top of the street. With a high wall surrounding the corner property to my left and a car park for flats opposite to my right, I wasn't nicking anyone's beloved parking space or loitering outside anyone's front room causing concern or unwelcome curiosity. My view stretched a fair way down the road, past 'Chestnuts' with its For Sale sign. The street lamps washed the pavements with traditional sickly orange light. There wasn't much traffic, this wasn't a rat run. One point in favour for my clients.

After half an hour I got out and had a stroll up and down for a closer look. The abandoned house across the road from 'Chestnuts' was in darkness and the business place deserted. Next-door to the Ecclestone's prospective home at 'Oakview' a people carrier sat in the driveway, immediate neighbours back from work. Walking further down the road I could smell fat – someone doing chips or a roast. My mouth watered.

Back in the car I settled in for a wait and watched dog walkers, couples, and students pass by. The students wore trousers wide as curtains, slung with heavy chains, some had their faces pierced and studded like biker jackets; one boy looked just like a hedgehog, his hair spiked all over his head and a long sharp nose. A dog barked on and off but not enough to call it a nuisance.

I listened to a few chapters of the latest George Pelecanos novel and at ten I ate my sandwiches: Cheshire cheese, basil and red onion, and drank some coffee from my flask.

My mobile rang as I was clearing up the crumbs. My friend Diane.

'Do you want to share a taxi on Saturday?'

'Can do.' We were going to a mutual friend's fortieth birthday party. 'How's the masterpiece?' Diane was making an original screenprint as a gift from the pair of us.

'Gorgeous. I might hang on to it and palm Chris off with one of my old posters.'

I laughed.

'You working?'

'Stakeout.'

'Ooooh.'

'Not a lot happening.'

'Good. Who are you staking out?'

'Potential noisy neighbours, undesirable elements. All quiet so far. So, Saturday what time?'

'Nine? She's doing a buffet.'

'Okay. Pick me up on the way. How are you?'

'Good. Got an interview at the Infirmary.'

'What for?'

'Artist in residence. Chance to do my own stuff and some for the hospital. They had a mosaics bloke last time, they might think textiles is a bit girlie.'

66

'That's it, think positive.'

Returning to my tape, I concluded that if anything was going to kick off it would be later when the pubs emptied. Didsbury Village, half-mile away was like a riot waiting to happen at the weekends. Hundreds of youngsters, set on having a good time, dead drunk and circulating through the pubs and bars on the prowl for fun, sex and oblivion. Taxi drivers steered clear. It was like town without the bus ride. Yet on Saturday mornings when everyone queued cheerfully in the deli or the fish shop, called at the library, browsed in the bookshop or gazed in one of the numerous estate agents you wouldn't have imagined it was the same place.

A car drove past me, a blare of sound. It parked in the yard in front of the apartments beyond 'Chestnuts'. The door banged and then things were quiet again. A plane took off, probably making more noise than anything so far. I jotted it down. The Ecclestones might need to know they'd get holiday flights going over throughout the summer, loud enough to prevent conversation in the garden and to wake you in the morning. It was only a few miles to the airport.

An hour passed and a dribble of people returned home. The only rowdy ones were two lads, obviously out of their skulls on something, kicking a can between them as they walked down the middle of the road. I watched them until they were out of sight. It was late now, my bladder was bursting and I could feel my back stiffening in reaction to the creeping cold. Time to call it a night. I switched the engine on, turned up the heater and pulled away.

As I drove into the side street a few hundred yards down on the left a movement caught my eye near one of the alleyways. A person stumbling, tripping. I was about to drive on, thinking it was someone the worse for drink, but as the figure stood upright the light from the street-lamp illuminated them. A woman, blonde curls, blood on her face and on her pale top. Eyes shut, face creased with distress. Adrenalin jolted through me like a fist in the belly. I stopped the car just a few yards past her and ran back to help.

'Are you all right?' Daft question I know but it was an opening.

She flinched at my voice, looked wildly about. Her arms were wrapped around her stomach. I was worried she was going to run off. I moved closer slowly and spoke quietly.

'What's happened, has there been an accident?' I couldn't see a crashed car but maybe someone had run her over.

She gave a jerky sob.

'I can take you to hospital.'

'No,' she shook her head, her voice was high with emotion.

'You're hurt.'

'I'm all right,' but then she staggered and I had to catch her to stop her falling.

'Come and sit down for a minute, my car's just here.'

She didn't resist and I steered her to the car and got her in the passenger side. The blood was coming from her nose and lip and from a cut high on her forehead. She was trembling violently, her teeth clattering, her breath jerky, a bubble of blood formed in one nostril and burst. I crouched beside her on the pavement, leaned over and pulled a J-cloth from the glove compartment. 'Here.'

She sniffed, took it and pressed it to her face.

'What happened? Was there an accident?'

'No.'

My stomach turned icy.

'Someone did this?'

She began to cry.

'I can call the police.'

'No,' she wept, 'please don't. I can't, please.'

She was frightened.

'Did you recognise them?'

'No.' She made an effort to pull herself together, wiping her nose and using her fingers to dry her eyes. 'I'm sorry. I just want to go home, get cleaned up.'

'Where were they?'

'I can't...' she broke off.

'If there's someone hanging around, attacking people...'

'It all happened so fast. I didn't see them, it was dark.'

'How many people?'

'One.'

'A man?'

She nodded.

'In the alley?'

Another nod.

'Did he take anything?'

'No.'

I swallowed. 'Just beat you up?' I wanted to ask if she'd been raped but it seemed brutal to say it so baldly. 'Did he try anything else?'

'No.' She started crying again. 'Shit,' she rocked to and fro and ran her hands over her hair a couple of times.

'You couldn't describe him? Age, height, clothing? Did he say anything, did you hear his voice?' I thought of the lads kicking the can. One of them perhaps? 'Where was he?'

'Please,' she raised her hands to the sides of her head, shutting me out. 'I can't think about it. I just want to forget it, leave it.'

I understood her reaction: the shock and terror displacing everything else. But if the attack wasn't reported then it would take that much longer for the bastard who'd attacked her to be caught. It might mean other attacks, other victims whose lives were suddenly damaged by random violence.

'Please can you take me home.'

'Of course.' I straightened up and sighed.

She lived nearby, Old Landsdowne Road which runs parallel to Severn Road. I parked where she told me to, in the middle of a row of terraced houses. There were lights on. 'Will there be someone there?'

'Yes.' She opened the car door.

'If you change your mind, about the police, I'd be happy to talk to them. This is my number.' I gave her my card. She took it without even glancing at it and pushed it awkwardly into her pocket.

'Can you manage?'

'Yes. Thanks.' Her voice was shaky.

She got out slowly, he must have hurt her body as well as her face. What with? Boots, fists, a bat?

I watched her until she'd opened the door and gone inside.

The brush with violence left me feeling hollow with fatigue but speedy too. I'd been hurt myself in the course of my work – the cases I investigate occasionally expose me to the risk of harm – but it must be even more traumatic when an attack comes from out of the blue with absolutely no reason.

Although my scars had healed there was still a visceral reaction to similar situations. Like a smell or a cherished melody that triggers powerful memories, the atmosphere that accompanies brutality awakened all those dreadful feelings from before. The childlike terror, the sick anxiety, the more complex reactions of guilt and depression. It all came flooding back and by the time I got home I too was tearful and trembling.

The house was quiet. Everyone in bed. I looked in on the kids. They were fast asleep. They'd want separate rooms before long. I wasn't sure how we'd do it. I speculated while I made cocoa and toast, lathered honey onto the toast and settled in the armchair in the kitchen. Swapping rooms about and dividing one of the bigger ones in half might be a possibility. Or waiting until Sheila, the lodger, moved out of her attic flat, which she was planning to do when she graduated. But without a lodger there'd be less money for rent and bills. Maybe Laura, Ray's girlfriend, would move into the flat with Ray, and then little Tom could have Ray's old room. I was trying to distract myself but I couldn't keep it up for long.

The heating had gone off and the room was cool so I kept my coat on. Digger sidled in and waited while I ate. When no crumbs came his way and I'd moved onto sipping cocoa he moseyed off again.

Images from the evening haunted me, the woman's teeth chattering, the silhouette of her stumbling, the bubble of blood in her nose. Would she think differently about reporting it in the morning? Maybe whoever she lived with would persuade her, give her some support.

I considered whether I should go to the police myself. What could I tell them? Precious little really. A lone woman had been attacked and beaten somewhere near Severn Road shortly before 11.40 p.m. She could give no description of her attacker and refused to report the crime. Sparse details but I decided I'd feel better passing them on to the police than not bothering.

How would I phrase this in my report to the Ecclestones? It may not have been the first time the man had struck. I'd have to see if the other residents, or even the police, could tell me anything.

My thoughts turned to the impasse I'd reached with Lucy Barker. She'd been adamant about talking to prickly Ian Hoyle herself. As yet he seemed the most likely culprit. Was she being foolish? If he held up his hands and confessed would that be the end of the matter? Or if she challenged him would he attack? He was already stressed, if he felt cornered he might act violently. Could I have done more to dissuade her?

In bed I cuddled a hot water bottle. Found it hard to sleep but I tried not to get wound up about it. At least I was warm and horizontal and safe at home.

Chapter Six

'That was Katy's mum on the phone. She wants us to pick Katy up today. I said she could stay for tea.'

Maddie gave a dull nod. Maddie looked like I felt; her face was pale and she had dark shadows beneath her eyes.

'Are you tired?'

'Yes.'

'Were you up late?'

'No. But Tom had that stupid mouse story on.'

'S'not stupid.'

'Go get your shoes,' I told them both.

It was a bitterly cold day. The April wind was coming from the north and the sky was heavy with moody clouds, dark grey and tinged with sulphuric yellow. I decided it would make sense to wait to hear from Lucy Barker about Ian Hoyle before attempting to talk to Carly Jowett.

The nearest police station is Elizabeth Slinger, on the far side of West Didsbury near to Princess Parkway and Southern

Cemetery. I called in there and waited for a while in the tiny reception area. Eventually I was invited through to a small, characterless interview room where young PC Tootall, with badly bitten nails and severe dandruff, heard me out. He took some notes but said he wasn't sure whether there'd be enough information especially without the victim's details to issue a crime number. He made a clumsy but well-intentioned speech about the police needing the co-operation of the public in order to do their job.

'Have there been any similar cases in the area?' I asked him.

'I've not heard of anything.'

That didn't really answer my question. 'Would it be possible to find out?'

'I'll check up on it if I get a chance later,' he said.

'Because people ought to be warned.'

He was noncommittal and we parted with a shared sense that my visit had probably been a waste of time.

Back at Severn Road the street felt different. The events of the previous night had tainted the place so I now felt the possibility of danger which I hadn't done before. The weather didn't help. I had to narrow my eyes against the wind and the gusts through the trees made it hard to hear.

At 'Oakview', next door to 'Chestnuts', the people carrier was parked in the drive. The Asian woman who answered the door was cautious at first. I had to explain to her twice why I wanted to ask her about the area then she studied my card closely. Finally satisfied, she invited me in. I was relieved I didn't have to do the interview shivering on the doorstep. She made tea and we sat in the front room which was obviously used as a study. It was very warm and I shed a layer of clothing. There was a desk and computer, books lined the walls and the place was peppered with art objects: several different puppets, musical instruments, sculptures and models made of metal, some blocky woodcuts.

They had lived in the house for twelve years. 'I work from home,' Mrs Mistry told me. 'I translate books so I'm here much of the time. It's not a bad area but you have to have good security. There are quite a lot of break-ins but that's true everywhere these days, isn't it? And I wouldn't walk around at night.'

My ears pricked up. 'Why's that?'

'It's not safe. Every week there's a mugging in the paper. I use the car.'

A depressingly familiar view. The world wasn't safe, the streets weren't safe. Strangers were a threat. The fear made us stop our children playing out, isolated us in our homes and cars. Never mind that unprovoked attacks like the one the night before were relatively rare, never mind that those most at risk from street violence were young men. Fear fed on itself, distorting our perception of risk.

'Have there been any incidents that you recall like that?'

'I'm sure there have but I can't remember all the ins and outs.'

'Anything recently?'

She shrugged.

'Have you had any problem with noise or anything else?'

'Not really.'

'What about the houses opposite? One's used for business.'

'Yes, people come and go in the daytime but there's no inconvenience. But next door to that, what an eyesore, isn't it?'

'Is it empty?'

'No, there's an old couple. We don't see them from one month to the next. I think they rent it. It really lets the area down.'

'Do you know who owns it?'

She shook her head.

'What about the flats on your side, next door but one? Are they let to students?'

'No, professional people. Nice people. There's a Resident's Association for West Didsbury,' she added. 'They organise things to try and improve the area. They work with the traders on Burton Road. It might be worth you talking to them. I've not heard of this before,' her tone became inquisitive, 'investigating somewhere for house buyers?'

'It's becoming more common. I think especially if someone has already had problems with noisy neighbours. The last thing they want to do is end up in the same situation again.'

'Well, tell them we're fine. My husband's at hospital all day, he's a cardiologist, and the children have homes of their own now. We're nice and quiet,' she smiled. 'Further down the road you might find it different.'

She began to tell me about her children and her new grandson. And eventually I had to interrupt her to get away. After leaving Mrs Mistry I went round to the flats but it looked like everyone was out at work. No cars about. And no answer when I tried the three bells.

I crossed to the offices that housed Severn

Insurance and Mannion and Shaw and spoke to a secretary there who seemed delighted to have her work interrupted. The two companies were linked, Mannion and Shaw were loss adjusters, and her boss spent much of the time visiting clients. She told me about a spate of burglaries they had suffered a couple of years previously.

'I blame the druggies,' she said.

She was probably right. Feeding a habit accounted for a good proportion of housebreaking in the city and the turf wars accounted for most of the shootings.

Their offices now had a comprehensive security system with sensors on doors and windows and the alarm was routed through to a security firm and the local police station. When I asked her if they still had problems she admitted things were much better. 'They know it's too much hassle here. The security firm are round like a shot.'

What about the run-down house next door? Did she know who owned it?

'Absentee landlords. They're based in London,' she said. 'We've been on at them for years to sort the place out, complained to the council, but nothing ever happens. There's a chimney up there and it's a miracle it hasn't come down and killed someone.'

'And there's an old couple living there?'

'The Smiths. You hardly ever see them about. Like recluses really. They ought to be in a home, somewhere they can be looked after properly. They can't manage. You'd know that if you met them.' She wrinkled her nose. 'The smell,' she pulled a face, 'I don't reckon they've had a change of clothes or seen a bar of soap for years. It's not right.'

I had a daft impulse to defend the Smiths; to point out their right to live as they pleased but I didn't know enough about their situation. Perhaps they did need help, would welcome it.

'Do they get any visitors? Social worker or anything?'

"Not that I've noticed. So, what's it like being a private detective? Do you follow people? Film them in secret?'

'Sometimes ... there's a lot of hanging about.'

'Humphrey Bogart – what was the guy he played?'

'Philip Marlowe.'

'I like them. Old black and white. My kids won't watch anything if it's black and white. Don't know what they're missing.'

Next door at the Smiths' the weeds were high, even on the old driveway. A rough trail through them to the door. Presumably for the mail that everyone got regardless: junk advertising and free papers. I knocked at the front door. Nobody answered. I picked my way round to the door at the side of the house. The whole thing had been boarded up so they must just have used the front entrance. At the back of the building an old garage had collapsed in on itself, sections of the roof timbers exposed and piles of brick smothered by creepers. Two sycamore trees on the boundary towered over the house, creating deep shade. They had spawned dozens of seedlings – many now taller than me. The rest of the ground was a jungle of brambles and couch grass. Someone had used the garden to dump rubbish. I could see the springs of an iron bedstead, a rotting mattress, a rusting supermarket trolley, old cans and bottles.

The windows at the back of the house were covered, some by curtains and one with sheets of yellowing newspaper. Moss and slime gave a green sheen to the red bricks. Depressing. If it was like this outside what would it be like inside? Living there wouldn't be good for the spirit, let alone what the body might suffer.

I tried again at the front, knocking loudly and calling through the letter box. 'Hello, Mr Smith, Mrs Smith, can I talk to you please? It won't take long.'

Nothing.

I looked in the letterbox but it had bristles to keep the draughts out so I couldn't see a thing. I put my ear to it and listened. The wind was still rattling through the trees so it was difficult. Pressing my fingers against one ear to block out the noise, I concentrated on the silence inside. I was sure they were in there. I could sense them. It was as if the house was holding its breath.

I took a diversion on my way back to the office retracing my route from the night before, past the spot where I'd seen the blonde woman fall, and on to her house. I stopped the engine and sat there looking at the place. What was I doing? Looking for some sort of tidying up of loose ends, hoping she'd choose that moment to reappear ready to report a crime and with a much clearer memory of what her assailant was like? But life's not neat. It doesn't come in tidy, easy-to-process chunks. Was she all right? Had the man attacked anyone else? Did he live round there? I took a deep breath, rolled my shoulders back and got on with my day.

Once I'd warmed up the office I typed up the bones of my report for the Ecclestones. Immediate neighbours seemed settled and on good terms. There were no disputes between them. There had been break-ins to houses on Severn Road but these had been more prevalent in previous years. Nevertheless residents had stressed the importance of good security. Referring to the assault I pointed out that details were sketchy and there was no evidence to suggest this was other than an isolated incident. The scruffy state of the house opposite may be cause for concern. I would make a couple more visits to Severn Road, to see what the neighbourhood was like on a weekend night.

I was hungry and was just clearing up before going home to eat when I got a call from Lucy Barker.

'I've seen Ian, straightened things out.'

Relief. I'd continued to worry that Lucy might be endangered as a result of tackling him.

'What did you say?' I sat down to listen.

'I started off gently, said I was sorry things were so difficult for him, with the baby and all. And how much I valued his friendship. I told him I was sorry that there'd been any misunderstanding between us.

'He brushed it off. He was much happier, they'd had a scan yesterday and apparently things look a lot better, much more hopeful. That must have been why he was so uptight when you met him, big day and all that.'

I wondered exactly what was wrong with the Hoyles' baby.

'Anyway, Ian was much more relaxed and I told him then how worried I was about the mail I'd had–'

'You told him there'd been letters?'

We'd agreed from the outset to keep the precise nature of the trouble under wraps.

'Well, I had to. And he was really concerned for me. I said the worst thing was waiting to see if there'll be any more; that dread of something else arriving, and I got quite upset. I know he'd have said then if he'd done it. He said was there anything he could do to help and had you got any ideas? He was very worried.'

Try as I might I couldn't imagine the man who'd seethed at me yesterday speaking these lines but if he was carrying a torch for Lucy and had good news about his child then maybe he'd undergone a personality change when she pressed the right buttons.

I still thought she was naive to think his concern meant he was innocent. Expressing sympathy and offering help didn't guarantee his innocence. Whoever had delivered that malicious death threat would be prepared to lie and play games to avoid detection.

'He even suggested I stay at the hotel for a bit if it would help.'

Very convenient.

'No. I don't think that's a good idea.' It could be a trap. As yet I hadn't figured out what else I could do to investigate Ian Hoyle but I didn't want Lucy in his clutches out of office hours. The lack of progress was frustrating. I'd known it would be hard when I took the case but that didn't lessen my desire to give it my best shot.

'I'm still planning to talk to Carly Jowett.'

'You still think she might be behind it?' She was surprised.

'I don't know. But it'd be silly to ignore the possibility. I need her contact details.'

'They're meant to be confidential.'

'Someone got yours.'

There was a sharp intake of breath. I felt ashamed of my comment. This woman had been frightened, she hardly needed such a harsh reminder. Maybe it was my low blood sugar making me irritable. 'I'm sorry,' I said.

'I'll explain the situation to Malcolm Whitlow – see if he can give me Carly's number.'

'Okay,' she said quietly.

Malcolm Whitlow hesitated for a moment but decided in my favour and gave me the phone number. 'If anyone asks,' he added, 'you didn't get it from me.'

'Fine,' I agreed. After all, I could always have found it by working my way through the Manchester telephone directory. This was simply a short-cut.

I sloped off home and made myself cheese and tomato on toast and cut a slab of Sheila's fruitcake. She's a great baker, from a generation who made cakes, biscuits, pies and scones once a week. Once we'd discovered she could do it we quickly came to an arrangement that we'd get supplies in and she, often assisted by Maddie, would do her stuff.

Being self-employed I don't need to sit at my desk and watch the clock. I'm my own boss and I love the flexibility (even though the downside is financial instability). So I decided not to go back to the office that afternoon; not enough to do. Instead I went to the supermarket. The weather affected my purchases. I managed to buy most of the basics we needed but also crumpets, muffins, tins of rice-pudding and tomato soup, ingredients for pies and stews. What I think of as the warming winter foods. I unloaded the boxes at home and put stuff away.

The freezer was icing up, the borders around each drawer were framed with dense curving edges of ice; moving them in and out led to small avalanches of crunchy snow from one level to the next. I could only just stuff the food in. It needed defrosting but it was such a tedious and messy job I always hung on until it was critical: when the door would no longer shut and the ice threatened to move, glacier-like, into the kitchen.

And while I pretended to ignore it, Ray was genuinely oblivious. He'd have to be suffering from frostbite before he realised that there was a polar ice cap emerging from the big white box where the burgers and chips were. He's like that: there are some household tasks that his brain just doesn't compute. Some of them I nag him about, determined to share responsibility but others are a trade-off for the things he does that I avoid. Like all the dog related stuff and fixing things that break or drop off or explode. I can change plugs, paint walls, strip floors and handle anything in the garden but I'm less confident when it comes to anything with rawl plugs and T-squares.

Katy, Maddie's classmate, came back from school with us. The two girls disappeared into the playroom when we got home and Tom went to play on the computer. I cleared up and transferred washing to the dryer and dry clothes to my bed for sorting out. Katy sought me out and asked to watch a video.

'Yes, which one?'

'Winnie The Pooh.'

'Fine. Maddie'll put it on for you.'

'She doesn't want to watch it.'

'Does she want something else?'

'Don't know.'

I went downstairs. No Maddie in the lounge. Nor in the playroom.

'Maddie,' I called out.

A pause, then, 'What?'

She was upstairs.

'Aren't you going to watch Winnie the Pooh with Katy?' I called.

'S'rubbish.'

For heaven's sake! What was she playing at now?

'I'll put it on for you,' I told Katy. She seemed happy enough.

Once I'd fast-forwarded past the adverts I left it running and went back upstairs, told myself to think of the exercise I was getting. Maddie was lying on her bed with a couple of soft toys. She and Katy got on so well usually. I sat on the edge of her bed. 'What's wrong?'

'I didn't say anything was wrong.'

'I know you didn't. Why don't you want to play with Katy?'

A shrug. 'I've got tummy ache.'

Give me strength! Maddie was a budding hypochondriac and it was treacherous trying to determine when she was genuinely ill and needed some treatment and when she just wanted attention. 'Sip some water.' I held out the cup from her bedside. She took a sip. I put my palms against her forehead and the back of her neck. No temperature.

'How's school?'

Another shrug.

'Any problems?'

Shrug.

If she was like this now, what fun would we have when she became a teenager? Maybe that was it! Maddie was entering adolescence several years early. We'd have grunts and shrugs, stormy looks and sudden tantrums for a few years and then she'd emerge fully mature and human again. Maybe.

'How about the pictures?' I said. She'd been wanting to go for ages. 'We could go on Saturday, invite Katy?'

'What's on?'

'I'll have to look in the paper. You coming down?'

She shrugged.

Maddie picked at her tea but had no problem with the chocolate mousse that followed. At half six Katy's mum Fiona arrived. I explained that Maddie had been a bit under the weather and mentioned the idea of a cinema trip. Katy was keen.

When Maddie was ready for bed we read some more from her library book. Tom listened too. I settled an argument about which tape to have by choosing one for them. An old favourite: Flat Stanley.

Sheila was back and I chatted to her while she made her tea. She was a mature student, studying for a degree in geology, and she was out a lot doing research for her current project.

My phone interrupted the chat.

Lucy Barker.

My stomach contracted as she spoke and the hairs on my arms pricked.

'I'm coming round,' I said. I glanced across at Sheila, who nodded. She would be in until Ray got back, he had gone off on one of his timber buying trips. 'You're at home?' I asked Lucy.

'Yes.'

'Can you stay there?'

'Yes.'

'I won't be long.'

I put my phone away, collected my bag and coat, her desperate words echoing in my mind, inflaming my imagination.

'*There's been another letter,*' she said, '*and a parcel.*' And her voice broke.

Chapter Seven

you *will* DiE soo*n* BItcH

I swallowed. Closed my eyes briefly. The same technique as before: a mishmash of letters and fonts.

'It was in your post box?'

'When I got back from work.'

'And a parcel?'

She was clutching one hand to her mouth, the other was wrapped in a tea-towel.

'Your hand?'

Her eyes filled with tears. She moved her head slowly from side to side.

'There was a razor blade.'

'Oh, my God.'

'And there was ... it's in there,' she gestured to the kitchen. 'I didn't know what to do.'

I went to look and she came with me, standing behind me as though I could shield her. On the counter was a manila jiffy bag, the sort lined with bubble wrap. No writing on it, the flap torn open. A razor blade and smears of blood on the counter top. The smell in there made me want to retch.

'It's dog shit,' she said.

'Oh, God! We have to report this.'

'No.'

I stared at her. I was surrounded by people refusing to involve the police.

'Show me your hand.'

She unwound the cloth. The top of two fingers were cut, as I looked fresh blood swelled in the thin slits.

'Jesus Christ. Look at that,' I told her. 'That's actual bodily harm.'

'No,' she squeaked and began to cry. I led

her into the other room, away from the foul stench.

'Have you got any plasters?'

She shook her head. Rummaging in my bag, I unearthed two dinosaur plasters. Not quite Lucy Barker's style but she let me put them over the cuts.

'Look, when you got the first letter, there was a chance it could have been a mistake, or someone wanting to get back at you for something and that would be the end of it. Then there was a direct threat.' I avoided using the words death threat though that's what it was. 'Now this. Not just to scare you but to actually hurt you. To cause physical damage. The police can do so much more: they can test for fingerprints, look at forensic evidence. My resources are very limited. Lucy, this is getting really nasty.'

She had stopped crying. She was very still. 'I was raped once,' she said, matter of fact, staring ahead. 'First term at college.'

Oh Jesus. I kept quiet.

'The tutor, the only person I told, she forced me to go to the police. It was like being raped all over again.' She looked at me, her blue eyes bleak. 'And they never even prosecuted him.'

This is different, I wanted to say. You can't

94

base what you do for the rest of your life on one experience, however bad. But then who was I to judge? I needed to acknowledge what she'd just told me. 'I'm sorry. That's awful. But please think about it. I would come with you, stay with you...'

'No,' she whispered.

I exhaled.

There was silence for a moment then I heard the front door bang and footsteps going upstairs.

'Do you think there could be any connection?' I asked her. 'With the rape?'

'No. The man's dead now, he died a couple of years ago. He jumped off a motorway bridge.'

I flinched.

She still sat staring into space, dull. An effort to protect herself from what we were talking about.

'Have you got a carrier bag?'

'Yes,' she blinked and got to her feet. In the kitchen she got me a bag. I used it like a glove to grasp the jiffy bag. I examined both sides but it was unmarked. Then I drew the carrier bag inside out, over the packet and tied it at the neck.

'And freezer bags something like that?' Intent on preserving some evidence, hoping

I could change her mind about the police, I manoeuvred the razor blade into one and put the letter in another.

'Let's have a drink.' I was keen to give her something practical to focus on to redirect her attention away from shock and introspection. I opened the window to air the kitchen and we took our drinks in the lounge.

'What time did you get in?'

'About seven.'

'That's later than usual?'

'I said I'd cover for Sheena, the night receptionist. She'd got parents' evening at her little boy's school.'

'And did you check the mail immediately?'

'Yes.'

'Tell me exactly what happened.'

'I picked it up.'

'What was on top?'

'The packet and that letter,' she nodded at the missive which lay unfolded on the coffee table, 'under that was a bank statement.'

'What time does your post usually come?'

'About eleven.'

So the hate mail was left afterwards. Between eleven and seven.

'What time did you speak to Ian Hoyle?'

She frowned, screwed up her eyes trying

96

to remember. 'Erm, just before lunch.'

Maybe this was his response. To up the ante?

'It can't be Ian,' she said. 'He was at work all day.'

'Lunch?'

'Hospitality visit. Conference organisers wanting a look round.'

'When did he leave?'

'He was working late.'

'Later than you?'

'Yes,' she turned to me, her words insistent and a little sharper now. 'Later than me. We all have to do it now and again. Why do you keep on about Ian? It's not Ian.'

'He couldn't have slipped away anytime today for an hour, forty minutes even?'

She gave a little snort, exasperated. 'It's not impossible but really...'

She was so sure. Not me though. A suspicious nature comes with the territory.

'Okay.' Supposing Ian Hoyle was in the clear, I thought again about the circumstances we had to go on. 'It's Wednesday, a week since the last letter?'

She nodded.

Was the timing significant? It could point to someone who was free on a Wednesday. 'Half-day closing.' There were still some

97

shops around Manchester that observed the old tradition of closing on a Wednesday afternoon to make up for staff having to work on Saturday. But the ones that did it tended to be small, local shops. 'Do you know anyone who works in a shop, on a high street, has Wednesdays off?'

She looked at me askance.

Okay it was a bit of a reach but I was fumbling in the dark. Someone hated her, hated her so much they'd gone to these lengths.

'Have you noticed anything different in the last day or two, anything odd, any friends or colleagues behaving out of character, suddenly avoiding you, anything off-balance?'

'No.'

'Any sense of someone watching you or being followed.'

'No.'

I ran my hands through my hair. Rubbed at my neck.

'What about the other people here. Who was in when you got back?'

'Just Adam, I think. There was just his car here.'

'Have you spoken to him?'

'No.'

'Hang on.'

I let myself out and crossed to the teacher's door. When he answered, minus kitten, I asked him if he'd noticed anyone bringing mail after the morning delivery.

'No. But I've only been back since five. Has something happened?'

'Yes, but I can't discuss it.'

He pulled a face. 'Have you tried the students?'

'Were they in?'

'Yes. I hear them moving about when they're home.'

I climbed the stairs and called on the students. They invited me in; I explained what had been going on. Had they been in during the day, noticed anyone coming?

'We have been in,' the man called Remi answered. 'We have been waiting for someone to come to fix the television.'

'He said he'd be here this afternoon,' his friend Daniel told me, 'so we are here all day and then he's not showed up.'

'We've been looking out sometimes too. No one came.'

Well, someone must have but not their repairman.

I thanked them and left a card with them as I had with the other clients asking them to call me if they noticed anything suspicious.

'Agatha Christie,' Remi said as he showed me out, 'I like the books very much.'

I smiled. I'd never read one.

'But Miss Marple is a bit older than you, yes?' He grinned.

'Careful, now.'

'Maybe she could find our television man,' he told Daniel.

I laughed.

The warmth I felt from the interchange faded rapidly as I reported back to Lucy. No leads from the neighbours. The mood between us was sombre and a bit prickly.

'Do you think I should stay at the hotel?' she asked me.

My instincts said no. If Ian Hoyle was involved then he might have engineered his offer to her and be preparing a trap, a third delivery here pushing her towards accepting his suggestion. No hate mail had been sent to the hotel and I was reasonably sure she was okay during working hours – hers was a very public role – but I didn't want her there after hours.

'No. Any friends who could put you up?'

'Not really. I don't ... people from work, they have families. I wouldn't like to intrude...'

It was an excuse. To mask a saddening

admission. She had no friends. She'd never mentioned anyone outside work except for Benjamin, and the people she trusted at work were colleagues and nothing more. Lucy would never be invited for a meal with Pam Hertz or a few drinks with Malcolm Whitlow.

'I could arrange for someone to come and stay here, if you wanted? A security guard. I can recommend him but you'd have to pay.' Brian was my partner at self-defence classes. He'd left his job with a local supermarket after playing host to several armed robberies and had set up on his own. He was a nice lad and I hoped he'd make a go of it.

'I don't want to stay here.'

'Bed and Breakfast, then. I know a place. It'll do for a couple of nights.'

'Okay. I'll get some things together.'

'I'm going to talk to Carly Jowett and if I've no luck there I'm going to try and trace the source of the letters used.'

And I wanted another go at Ian Hoyle but I didn't mention that.

'Won't that be difficult?'

'Probably, yes. There's someone I can ask about it. I think the trouble is, even if we trace the newspapers, like I said before, if they're freely available over the counter then it doesn't narrow the search much. And if nothing has turned up before then I'll keep watch on this place next Wednesday; maybe there's a pattern.'

There must be some history behind it, I thought. Totally random vendettas are so rare. It was much more likely that Lucy Barker knew her enemy. That they had some reason, however skewed, to want to frighten her, threaten her.

She seemed so alone: fiancé dead, no friends, family across the other side of the planet. I hadn't warmed to Lucy Barker but I felt sorry for her, for the position she was in. No one but me to share her anxiety, to offer solace.

'We don't know who's behind this or how serious it is but I think there are some basic precautions you should take.' I tried to sound businesslike, not wanting to alarm her unduly with the prospect that someone might follow through on the threats they'd made. She looked at me and I glimpsed a flash of impatience in her eyes. Perhaps it came from the strained atmosphere, our disagreement about involving the police. Or maybe she had heard all this before, after the rape. Had been doing it ever since:

always alert to personal safety, always minimising risks. If so, she must find me patronising.

'Stop me if you know all this.'

'No, carry on.'

We went through all the obvious areas: answering the door, travelling, parking. Avoid isolated, ill-lit areas, if confronted: run, scream, avoid eye-contact. Be on the look out for anyone following you. Trust your instincts. Our bodies are often the first to sense danger, before our minds cotton on. And they are very accurate early warning systems.

I gathered up the freezer bags. But there was no way I was going to hold on to a jiffy bag full of dog shit. 'I'll get rid of the package.' I moved to the kitchen.

'No, I will.' She hurried ahead of me, picked up the carrier and took it outside to the bins. I shut and locked the window and then waited while she packed a bag. We'd need to think about a system for monitoring her mail but it could wait till the next day; she was obviously shattered.

We drove in convoy to the Bed and Breakfast. I saw her checked in. Back in my car I sat and let the tension drain from my arms and my shoulders, took a couple of deep breaths. I was uneasy. Something was nagging at me, something about the case. I tried to pin it down by scrolling through all the elements and hoping for a gut reaction, a clenching that told me where my concern lay: the hate letters, the razor blade, the person behind them, Lucy Barker's refusal to go to the police, Ian Hoyle, the rape disclosure, my failure to make progress? Nothing clicked. But something lurked, veiled beneath the surface, something that disturbed me. I'd told Lucy Barker to listen to her instincts and knew I should follow my own advice. But how could I when all I had to go on was a vague sense of disquiet. How could I act on that? Resign from the case? Break client confidentiality and confide in the police? No.

The unpleasant feeling remained with me while I drove home. I put on an old Astrid Gilberto tape, plenty of lilting melodies and lyrics in Portuguese. Nothing too demanding or strident. Hoping in vain that it might soothe away my worries.

Chapter Eight

Thursday morning I rang Carly Jowett and the woman who answered told me Carly was at work. Had she got the number? She had. 'You'll be lucky if they answer. They never bloody answer it, not for ages. Kwik Save, Slow Save more like.' She gave a hacking laugh at her incredibly witty joke. 'Have you got a pen?'

'Yes.'

She reeled it off. 'She's a couple of gaps on Saturday if you're sharp about it.'

That threw me.

'Gaps?'

'Appointments – for the nails.'

I mumbled a thank you and rang off. Gaps on Saturday? A second job for Carly Jowett?

The phone rang out at the supermarket till I was sick of waiting. I looked the place up in the phone book and soon found the address for the store, the one in Northenden. Northenden starts just south of the Mersey on the way to Wythenshawe. In rush hour it's horrendous as the road leads to the M60 and other motorways. I'd missed the worst of the traffic. I drove over the river, casting a glance at the weir under the flyover.

In the store I approached a lad unloading a load of tinned goods on the first aisle and asked for Carly.

'She's on her break, I think,' he said, 'hang on.' He wandered down the aisle a bit and shouted over to the woman on the checkout. 'Carly on her break?'

'What?'

'Carly – on her break?'

'Yeah. Out back.'

He turned to me. 'Big doors, car park, round the back.'

I went out and followed the car park round to the loading doors at the back of the store. Here, a young girl, with blue hair extensions and nails painted like miniature seascapes cradled a cup of tea and sucked on a cigarette.

'Carly?'

She swivelled her head to look my way but moved nothing else. 'Yeah.'

'Have a word?'

'What about?' Her brow creased.

Sullen was the first word that sprung to mind.

'I'm working at the Quay Mancunia Hotel.'

She reared her head back, on the defensive.

'Assessing management practice. Would you mind answering a few questions about your time there?'

'Yes, I bleeding would. Bloody cheek of it.'

Damn. I tried to spark her interest. 'There have been complaints about a senior manager, I can't go into details but your view would be extremely useful. All in complete confidence of course. And I can offer you a small payment for your time – interrupting your break.'

'Yer doing what?' She scowled, took another drag on her cigarette, flicked her eyes at the fiver I held out.

'Investigating the management. There have been some complaints to the union.'

'Not surprised.'

'How do you mean?'

'Dictators,' she said. 'Treat you like a kid or summat.'

I nodded as though this had been exactly what I'd been hearing. She took the money, pocketed it.

'Who was your manager?'

'Lucy Barker. Right snob she was. You know what she says. "A smile doesn't cost anything, Carly", expects you to grin all day like a bleeding hyena. And she's always picking on you, personal stuff, not about your work. What colour your tights are and how you've done yer hair.'

I was pretty sure Carly's hair hadn't been blue braids during her stint on Quay Mancunia reception.

'Worse than school.' She had a drink.

I nodded energetically. 'She wasn't very popular then?'

'Not with me she weren't.' She drew hard on her cigarette and held her breath while the nicotine worked its magic. 'Mind you,' she blew a stream of smoke out, 'I reckon she were a bit demented. She'd been engaged to this bloke, he'd been killed in a car crash and she's always on about it. She was in the car with him, he died in her arms. Perfect couple they were. I'm not being tight but I got sick of hearing about him. Like, get over it will you.'

'Intense.'

'Yeah.'

She didn't like the woman but did she dislike her enough to start a hate campaign against her?

She took a swallow from her cup. 'And she'd get all neurotic, running off to Mr Hoyle every chance she got about stuff that didn't matter, like someone being five minutes late...'

Guess who, I thought.

'...or the front desk being left in a mess.'

'What was he like?'

'Not bad. Didn't have much to do with him, really. I reckon Lucy Barker fancied him.'

I raised my eyebrows and she nodded at me. 'She thought no one knew but I could tell. He'd not been married long, baby on the way,' she pulled a face. 'I think he told her where to get off...'

Or the other way around?

'...suddenly it's all long silences and they're never in the same room together.'

Carly had assumed Lucy was making the running. Why? One glaring contradiction struck me and I voiced it. 'I thought she was still in a state about her late fiancé?'

'I know. State about everything.'

'How do you mean?'

'Her whole life, it was one tragedy after another, like living in a soap-opera. Acts as if no one else has ever had any bad luck.'

Carly sounded harsh. Perhaps she too had seen hard times but didn't confide in people so readily and was scathing of those who did.

'What sort of things?'

'She had meningitis when she was little, nearly died and her grandfather was killed in one of them IRA bombings, then her mother had a stroke and she had to do all the housework, and her brother was a junkie, sold the telly and all their things, and the car crash of course. She'd slip them in when she were talking to us. Like, I didn't want to know.'

'Why do you think she did that?'

She gave another shrug. 'Maybe she thought I'd feel sorry for her.'

I wondered if Lucy had told Carly about the rape?

'I've heard there were some falling's out at the hotel, between staff? Anything like that when you were there?'

'No, apart from what I said about Mr Hoyle.'

'Anyone making trouble?'

'No. She played people off a bit.'

'Miss Barker?'

'Yeah. Say one thing to one person and something different to another. Stirring it. Little things, though. Sort of unsettled everybody. Sly, she is.'

'Can you give me an example?'

She thought. Grimaced. 'It's hard to remember.'

It wasn't anything other colleagues had mentioned.

'I didn't trust her,' she blew out another stream of smoke.

Which was rich coming from Carly given her predilection for nicking stuff.

'What about Pam Hertz, what was she like?'

I couldn't imagine Carly taking to the slightly bossy style of the housekeeping manager.

She wrinkled her nose. 'Strict. But she wasn't that bad when you got used to her. The housemaids liked her.'

'And Malcolm Whitlow?'

Who had given her the sack.

She flushed, took a final drag of her fag and tossed the butt into a pool of spilt milk where it sizzled and died. 'Dunno,' she hunched her shoulders, more uncomfortable now.

'You like it better here?' I changed the subject.

She smiled, the first time in our conversation and her eyes sparkled with glee as she did. 'You joking? I'm setting up on my own soon. Nails.' She wriggled the seascape fingers at me. 'I'm going for a business grant, for small businesses in the community, they help you out in your first year. Be my own boss. Here I do ten till eight and it's a miracle if I get any lunch. Depends who turns in.'

'Do you work every day?'

Her eyes narrowed and she cocked her head in enquiry.

'Were you here yesterday?' I said bluntly.

'Who wants to know?' Suspicion flashed in her eyes and her lips tightened.

'It's something else I'm looking into. There's been a bit of trouble.'

'What's it got to do with me?'

'Nothing. If you were here.'

'Fuck off.' She said sharply. She turned to go. Wheeled back. ''Course I was fuckin' here. I don't know what your game is but I haven't got anything to hide. Come on. I'll fuckin' prove it.' She marched off and I followed my cheeks glowing.

In the store she strode up to the till where another cashier was working and three customers queued.

Hands on hip she called to the woman.

'Yesterday, Gemma, what hours did I do?'

'Ten till eight, didn't yer?' The girl paused in swiping the goods.

'And when did I have my lunch?'

Gemma's face went slack as she groped

for the memory. The queue waited all ears.

'Ah,' her face brightened. 'Yer didn't have any. Just a fag break, Nicky weren't in. You clocked it up as overtime.' Gemma nodded and reached for the next item.

Carly glared at me – satisfied?

'Thanks,' I said.

'And don't fuckin' come back,' she said.

A gasp from the queue.

I fled.

Okay it had been embarrassing but I'd got the information I needed. Carly hadn't been behind the poison pen letters. Next on the check-alibis list was Ian Hoyle, never mind what Lucy kept telling me. I don't often have to be duplicitous with my clients, and I recognised it was a bad sign that I didn't trust her judgement. But all I needed to do was to establish his movements for the previous day, surreptitiously so she didn't hear about it. I thought through my approach while I drove back to my office. The weather was warmer than it had been. The previous day's wind had dropped and spring sunshine made the cherry blossom dazzle on the trees that lined the roads.

Ian Hoyle hadn't been pleased to talk to me the first time around; he had no reason for even agreeing to see me now. I'd have to convince him it would be to his advantage to see me. Or give him no choice in the matter.

Chapter Nine

I rang Lucy at the hotel to see how she was.

'Okay, but I'm owed some leave, I'm going to take tomorrow off and make a long weekend of it. Get away for a bit.'

'Sounds good. Better a B&B somewhere a bit more scenic. Let me know where you are. I can ring you if anything comes up.'

Then I called an old friend of mine, a journalist and something of a techno-geek called Harry. Did he know anyone who could help me identify the fonts and eventually the publications that had been used to construct the poison pen letters?

'But not the police?'

'Not an option at this stage.'

'Hmmm. Are they common fonts?'

'I don't know Harry, I haven't tried comparing them to anything myself. I'd rather get an expert to do it – they could probably look at it and reel off a list of papers without blinking. Are there people who do that?'

'Will be, case of finding them. Leave it with me, I can think of one bloke might know where to try.'

After the call I transferred the letters to my file.

I was still no nearer deciding on my opening lines for Ian Hoyle so I went swimming. I go a couple of times a week. It's the only exercise I get apart from riding my bike and the work-out we do at self-defence on Friday nights. On a regular basis I promise myself that I'll do more, try running or the gym as well, but it never comes to pass.

Withington Baths are housed in a classic Victorian building. The pools are small, a bit shabby but the staff are friendly and the place is convenient. I'd never swim at all if it meant traipsing to the flash new Aquatics Centre; it would take too big a chunk out of my day to travel into town.

I said my hellos to the lifeguards and got changed, exchanged greetings with the regulars in the water and began my half-hour. Counting lengths had got pretty boring so I just went by the clock instead. I swam as hard as I could and after the first few lengths I was in my stride. On autopilot, my thoughts returned to Lucy.

She'd certainly had a rough life. Added to the rape and her fiancé's death in her arms, there was also her grandfather's violent death, her brother's drug addiction and her mother's stroke. How old had Lucy been then? And why hadn't Lucy gone when they had all emigrated? Had she met Benjamin by then? And planned her future with him? Now she'd lost that too. Carly Jowett had resented Lucy talking about these events but with all Lucy had gone through there must have been times when other people's trivial concerns grated on her. Perhaps times when Lucy had wanted to put things in perspective. But confiding in her colleagues had not always been welcome. Some found her too intense – like the assistant who had asked for a transfer. Others probably felt uncomfortable; work wasn't necessarily the right place to air private tragedies.

At the end of my stint I floated on my back. I savoured the way the sounds of the pool were muffled by the water and let my limbs, aching and warm from the effort, relax. When I breathed I could feel how the swim had stretched my lungs.

The pool was emptying of swimmers in

time for the schools who use it either side of lunch. I did a lazy backstroke down to the deep end and climbed up the concrete steps. I stood at the edge, in the centre and stuck my toes just over the rim. I bent my knees, focused, took a deep breath and dived. Down, down, bubbles streaming about me, a moment of disorientation before I rose breaking the surface. Exhilarating. A rush of physical satisfaction. The happy hormones rewarding me for exercising.

As I changed, I thought about Maddie who didn't seem happy and the woman who had been beaten up the other night. I imagined her trying to cope; not just with what had happened to her but what might. That dread anticipation. My sense of well-being shrank a bit. Come on, I told myself, just do what you can. And whatever lay ahead it would be easier to tackle it now I was feeling that little bit fitter.

After lunch I tried Ian Hoyle hoping that Lucy Barker wouldn't take the call and recognise my voice. The woman I spoke to told me Mr Hoyle was in a meeting all afternoon. Erring on the side of caution I chose not to leave a message.

The next call I got was from school. The secretary was ringing on behalf of Maddie's teacher who wanted to see me; could I get to school quarter of an hour earlier than usual?

'Yes,' I said, feeling a rush of anxiety swill through my stomach. 'Is there something wrong?'

I knew it couldn't be an accident or anything because they'd have said straight away.

'I don't know, I was just asked to make the appointment with you.'

Forty-five minutes and I couldn't bear to sit and stew. I'd be better off working than brooding. There was time to pay another random call on Severn Road for the Ecclestones.

The weather was fine but getting colder. The forecast was for a cold snap over the weekend, with temperatures dipping below freezing and snow on the hills. This had sparked more debate on the increasingly mercurial nature of the weather and the impact of global warming.

I drove the length of the street. It was pretty deserted. Some workmen were clearing rubbish into one of the skips at the big detached place and a postal worker slowly steered her bike with its front tray of letters from one house to another.

I parked outside 'Chestnuts' and checked the time. I was startled by rapping on my car window. It was Mrs Mistry from 'Oakview'. I wound it down.

I thought it was you, I was wondering whether to ring. There've been a whole lot of break-ins.'

'When?'

'Last night. They tried here, the window round the back, but the alarm went off. We had the police round and they said there'd been three other attempts, all along here. They think it was kids because they weren't very professional. Maybe vandals. They let tyres down on some of the cars. And the house further down, the one near the corner, being renovated...'

I nodded. The one with the skips.

'...they got in there and made a real mess. It makes you wonder what the parents are thinking of when the children are out all hours running riot.'

'You've not had this sort of trouble before? The vandalism?'

'No. The police say there's been a lot of it up Burton Road, could be the same lot.'

'Was anything taken?'

'A video and a laptop at one house.'

Vandals or burglars. The two were quite

different. Vandals were out for kicks and easily drew attention to themselves. Burglars wanted to come away with goods they could sell on, they weren't in the business of doing anything to delay their chance of getting away. One laptop wasn't much of a haul in a street like Severn Road.

'Would you like to come in for a drink?' she offered.

'No thanks, I'm not going to be here very long, just a quick visit.'

A couple of minutes later and I saw an old woman bundled up in layers of tatty clothes shuffle very slowly out of the driveway opposite and onto the pavement. The reclusive Mrs Smith. She had long grey hair which stuck out beneath an ugly, brown knitted hat. I got out of the car and approached her.

'Mrs Smith, hello.'

She glared at me. Up close I could see that a cataract had turned one of her pupils into a milky disc, her skin was crepey and the colour of whey except for her nose which was a mass of purple veins. She stank; the rank smell of desperate poverty. I tried not to breathe it in. Now I was facing her I didn't know what to say I heard myself babbling: 'Is everything okay with the house? Only some of the neighbours think the landlord should be made to sort it out, repair it properly. Have you seen the landlord recently?'

She shook her head but it was a dismissal not an answer. She had no socks on and the stitching had rotted in the men's shoes she wore exposing the side and heel of her foot which was rimmed with dirt.

'Is there anything you need?' I carried on.

'No,' she said hoarsely. She waved me aside, her hands red and blotchy, and resumed her shuffle.

Pointless to persist. I crossed back to the car and got in. I watched her make her way to the corner in my rearview mirror. What could I do? I wasn't a social worker and the woman hadn't wanted my interference. Had she got a social worker? She looked sick, she wasn't dressed for the cold weather. Surely the authorities should give her some support. Maybe they could put pressure on the landlord to sort the house out.

I rang Rachel, my social worker friend and asked for her opinion.

'People get referred by their GPs, or family, sometimes neighbours. They may already be in the system.'

'Could you check?'

I gave her the name and address.

'First names?'

'Don't know.'

'You do pick them don't you, Sal ... Smith, could take forever.'

'What if they're not getting help? Can you get someone to come and see them?'

'We can try but if they won't open the door, if they don't want to see anyone, we can't force them. Not unless they're creating a nuisance or breaking the law. Sometimes the GP's a better bet. When people hear we're from Social Services they think we're going to cart them off soon as look at them.'

'Will you check then?'

'Yep. Can't do anything against people's wishes you know. I remember one case–'

'Rachel, sorry, I have to go.' Rachel was gabby. The only way to deal with her was to stop her before she got started.

'Fine.'

'See you at Chris's party on Saturday.'

'Great, see you there.'

On my way to school I drove past Mrs Smith. She was on her way back clutching a small, thin blue carrier bag in one hand. She'd been for provisions. Bread or milk maybe. Whatever it was it wouldn't last two of them all that long. I wondered how they managed for food, generally. According to the neighbours they were rarely seen, so how did they do the shopping?

Both the head teacher, Mrs Tewkes, and Maddie's class teacher, Miss Dent, were waiting to see me. Once I'd sat down Mrs Tewkes began to speak. 'Thank you for coming in. I'm afraid we've had a number of incidents involving Maddie and we felt we needed to discuss them with you, and see what sort of support she might need.'

My face burned. 'What sort of incidents?'

'Aggressive behaviour in the playground and other problems in class.' She gestured for Miss Dent to continue.

'Maddie has not been behaving well, I'm afraid. She's falling behind with her work and she's disrupting other pupils.'

This was so unlike Maddie I could barely believe what I was hearing.

'I'm afraid Maddie has spoilt some of the other children's work and this morning she reduced another child to tears with name-calling.'

I was appalled. 'It's not like Maddie at all...'

'Exactly,' said Mrs Tewkes. 'We were wondering if there has been anything happening outside school that might explain the change in her behaviour?'

At home, she meant.

'No, nothing.' I sounded defensive. 'She's been moody at home...' My mind raced about as I spoke trying to think of any major crisis I'd managed to overlook, '...she's been a bit flat and she wasn't keen on coming back to school after the holidays but she often says that at the start of term and then once she's back it's all okay again.'

'She's not said anything at home about these problems?'

'No.' I'm a bad mother, my child can't talk to me. 'Obviously, I've asked her whether there's been anything wrong – with her being a bit sulky – but she's not said anything.'

'I don't want to dwell too much on what's happened,' said Mrs Tewkes, 'I think we should put our energies into helping Maddie improve her behaviour.'

I did want to dwell though. This was all news to me and I wanted to know all the details of Maddie's outbursts and who she picked on. But I didn't feel I could ask them at that point.

'There must be something behind it all though,' I said. 'Nothing's changed in class has it?'

Miss Dent shook her head.

'She's not moved groups or anything?'

'No.'

'What I suggest,' Mrs Tewkes said, 'is a positive discipline plan. Miss Dent will talk to Maddie after the end of school today and tell her what behaviour we expect from her, go over the school rules. Then we'll use a simple sheet to mark acceptable behaviour for each session of the school day. If at the end of a week Maddie has responded well we can ease up on the close monitoring.'

'And if she doesn't?'

'We'll talk again but with most children who stray a little this is quite a successful strategy. We'd like you to reinforce what we're doing at home, reward positive behaviour, give her lots of praise...'

What did she think I did? Put her down all the time or hit her? For an awful moment I wanted to lash out. I nodded in agreement. 'Of course,' I just kept the edge from my voice. 'I'd like to know a bit more about the incidents you mentioned. The aggression...'

'Mainly verbal. Maddie has been name-calling, jostling another member of class, kicking, spitting.'

'Spitting?' I found it hard to credit. Maddie could be awkward, stubborn but until then her behaviour at school had been exemplary. What was happening to her? I wasn't cross with her, I was worried. 'Who was she calling names?'

'Carmel.' A little girl who was overweight and wore glasses.

'Oh, no. I'll do what I can at home but I'd like to know immediately if there's any more trouble.'

Miss Dent nodded.

'I wouldn't worry too much,' Mrs Tewkes tried to reassure me. 'We all know that Maddie is a lovely little girl, hard-working, liked by her classmates. I'm sure this is a temporary upset and she'll respond well to some firm limits. If you want to talk again, any worries, anytime.' She smiled.

I tried to smile back but there was no heart in it. I was too upset.

I went and took my place in the playground feeling extremely awkward. The implications of what I'd heard began to sink in. Maddie would have had her face on the sad face board; an indignity she would have hated. She had always spoken with horror and great disdain about the naughty ones who featured there. Now she'd been labelled naughty. And she'd have had to go in the timeout room while the rest of the school played out.

Tom's class came out and he ran up full of chatter about a visit from the Bugman. I half listened. I spotted Carmel, her grandad collecting her. I hated the thought that my little girl had been cruel to her. She's not like that, I kept thinking but I was wrong. Maybe she hadn't been like that in the past but she'd changed. I barely dared look at the other parents, I knew how fierce I'd feel if it had been Maddie on the receiving end.

While Mrs Tewkes did door duty, Miss Dent had her talk with Maddie. When Maddie finally came out, looking smaller and younger than I usually imagined her, I felt a surge of affection and a lurch of inadequacy. Why couldn't I make it all better for her? Why wasn't loving her enough?

Chapter Ten

Ray came home while I was clearing up the children's tea. He'd been helping a friend to fit some wooden units in his kitchen.

I seized the opportunity to tell him all about Maddie.

'Maddie? You're joking!'

His response was exactly what I needed to hear. 'I know. I mean she's been really moody since they went back but this ... and I don't know what's behind it all. There must be something, some reason.'

'Have you asked her?'

'No, not outright. I want to sit down and have a proper talk with her on Saturday.'

He blew out breath noisily.

'You think that's a bad idea?'

'No, just don't envy you.'

'Tom hasn't said anything to you?'

'No, he's probably not even noticed.'

I smiled.

'Well, you know what he's like.'

I did. He was a contented little boy and very little ruffled his cheerful, energetic character. He didn't tend to pick up on other people's moods like Maddie did.

'I think it must be something at school.'

'So what did the teachers actually say?'

I went over it all again in detail. Ray listened and made a few comments, it was helpful to share it with him.

'I heard back from TXL,' he said as I set the table. 'The IT interview.'

'And...' I turned to face him, I knew he really wanted a stable job.

'Got it!' His eyes danced and a smile softened the rather harsh look his moustache gave him.

'Brilliant! Half time?' Already my mind was racing ahead to implications for childcare.

'Think so. I've got to go in and talk about the details with someone there. There's some scope for working from home too, at least for some of the time.'

'Ray, that's great. Are you pleased?'

'Ye-e-es,' he looked askance. Of course he was.

Ray whistled and Digger leapt up from the spot by the armchair where he'd been dozing. Ray fetched his lead and Digger did his kangaroo routine. They set off for the park.

I didn't even try talking to Maddie until bedtime and then I kept it brief. I sensed that anything more coming on top of being cautioned by Miss Dent would be counter-productive. A proper talk could wait until the weekend.

As I supervised her cleaning her teeth and while Tom was in the bedroom getting his pyjamas on, I simply said that Miss Dent had told me she was doing a behaviour sheet and that I knew she'd do really well. 'It sounds like things have been hard for you this week but I'm sure it'll get better.' Her arm froze. She looked at me via the mirror, a guarded expression on her face.

'I love you very much,' I planted a kiss on her head. She didn't say anything, just resumed brushing her teeth.

'And I want you to be happy. Anything that's worrying you, you can tell me about it, anytime. Doesn't matter what it is, we'll sort it out.'

She spat into the sink and bent to drink from the tap.

She tapped her brush, straightened up. 'Can I stay up and watch *EastEnders?*'

I hesitated. Myself, I never watched the programme but most of Maddie's classmates seemed hooked on it.

'You'll have to go straight to bed when it's over.'

'I will.'

'Go down now and I'll think of something to tell Tom.'

I settled with Maddie in the lounge; it seemed important to sit with her while she watched it. She was cross-legged on the floor, leaning back against the sofa where I sat. When I stroked her head a couple of times and she didn't shake me off, I took it

130

as a good sign.

She went off to bed without prompting when the programme finished. Tom was already asleep and I turned off the tape he'd been listening to and dimmed his night light. Maddie had a light by her bed which stayed on all night; she would never sleep in the dark.

Waking in the night, to go to the toilet, I fell over Maddie who had dragged her duvet across the landing and was curled up outside my bedroom door.

'What are you doing there?' I whispered.

'I had a nightmare.'

'Why didn't you come in and get me?'

'I thought you'd be cross.'

I sighed. 'You should go back to bed now.'

'Can I come in your room?'

I didn't argue. She could sleep on my chaise longue but I refused to keep the light on.

'That's all right,' she said. 'I don't need the light on if you're here.'

I'd an awful vision of having to share my room with her for years on end – and it only just felt like I'd weaned her off climbing in with me as it was – but I dismissed my fears. These were unusual times and if a few nights together helped her feel happier then I could live with that.

Lucy Barker was off work on Friday – taking a long weekend – so I didn't have to worry about her seeing me if I turned up at the hotel. I'd decided the most effective way to get to see Ian Hoyle was to turn up unannounced. Believing if I tried to make an appointment he'd probably refuse.

There was no problem getting past reception; I tagged onto a group in business suits who were just leaving the circular lobby and heading for the conference suites. I remembered the way to Ian Hoyle's office and hoped he'd be in and alone. My wishes were granted but he was not pleased to see me again. And that's putting it mildly.

He looked up from his desk and his eyes expanded with astonishment and then narrowed with irritation. 'I'm sorry to bother you again but I wouldn't be here if it wasn't important.'

'What the hell...' He rose, his cheeks darkening. 'You can't just walk in here. Get out.'

'Mr Hoyle, please...'

'If you don't get out now, I'll have you thrown out.'

'If you can just answer one question...'

He pressed a switch on the console on his desk. 'Malcolm, it's Ian. There's an intruder in my office.' The muscles in his jaw twitched.

'Would you prefer I go to the police? Ask them to look into all this?'

'All what?' he demanded. 'Yes, go to the police, what the hell do I care? It's nothing to do with me.'

That threw me a bit.

'Isn't it? Lucy Barker rejects your advances but you don't like being turned down. Next thing she's getting hate-mail.'

'My advances?' He looked horrified.

The door opened and Malcolm stood there, body tensed, face alert, the jaw set between his teddy-boy sideburns. 'An intruder?' he asked in his gravelly voice. He looked at me and back at Ian Hoyle. Silence.

'I'll talk to them directly then,' I bluffed. Keeping my tone light. I took a step.

Ian Hoyle sighed. 'Malcolm, it's okay. Misunderstanding.'

'You're sure?' Malcolm frowned, ran his hand over his pate. Uncertain as to how he should respond and obviously embarrassed to realise I was the intruder.

'Yes. Sorry.'

Malcolm made a huffing sound and grimaced, deepening the creases in his face. He knew there was more to it, and that he wasn't being told. 'Right, then, I'll leave you to it,' his voice thick with resentment. He left the room.

'Lucy Barker told you I made advances?' Ian Hoyle asked. His eyes glittered and I could sense his pent-up fury. I remained standing, ready to flee the room if he let rip.

'Yes.'

He laughed, a peculiar, humourless squeal.

'Are you saying it didn't happen?'

'Is it any of your business?' He ran a hand across the dark stubble on his jaw.

'Only if it relates to the threats she's received. And at the moment...'

'Listen – Lucy was the one making advances, coming on to me. She wouldn't take no for an answer.' He said vehemently, his mouth taut as he chewed out the words.

I blinked. It was a classic situation. A messy, relationship, both parties misreading the signals. Each blaming the other. Diametrically opposed views of what happened. 'So you decided to frighten her off?' I spoke calmly, inviting an admission.

'Jesus Christ!' he exploded. I backed away a step. 'No, no! I didn't.' He raised his hands as if he'd grasp his own head then let them fall in exasperation. 'God.'

'Mr Hoyle, when Lucy spoke to you about this on Wednesday...'

He made another strangled noise and shook his head, a rictus of incredulity on his face. 'Lucy didn't speak to me on Wednesday. Not about this or anything else.'

'You were here? In work?'

'Why?'

'It would help remove any suspicion.'

His face tightened again. He was weighing up whether to chuck me out, I was sure. 'Why should I help you?'

'Stop me bothering you?'

He leant over his desk and flicked a switch again. I braced myself for Malcolm to be summoned but I didn't need to.

'Rhona, can you bring the diary in?'

We waited in silence for a couple of moments, the air crackling with tension, and then the door opened.

A petite woman in a black trouser suit came in and handed a large diary to him.

'The meeting with C.M. Training, Wednesday – when did that finish?' he asked her coolly.

She stood at his side, peered at the book open across his arms. 'About quarter past four. We ran over and the marketing meeting started late as a result.'

'So, I was back to back all day.'

'Yes,' she looked confused.

'And my first meeting?'

'Eight-thirty.'

'Lunch?' I said.

His head moved, a little jerk of impatience and he turned to Rhona.

'Working lunch,' she said. 'Conference clients visiting. We were back to back all day like you said. I'm still doing the minutes.'

'Thanks.'

She made a moué, took the diary from him and left.

'Thank you,' I said. I thought he was telling the truth. Either that or he'd gone to elaborate lengths to instruct Rhona to give him an alibi and tamper with the diary and schooled her in acting it all out perfectly. He'd had no chance to bring Lucy's latest ugly delivery to her flat.

'Lucy, she...' He shook his head, folded his arms deciding not to confide in me further.

'She thought you were interested in her...'

'God knows what she thought. I hate to imagine what's going on in that head of hers.' He paused then tilted his head back exposing his Adam's apple before lowering it and looking straight at me. 'Do you know what she did when I made it clear that I wanted nothing more to do with her?' His eyes were shiny with fury. 'She threatened to ring my wife and tell her we were having an affair.'

I swallowed. Thought of what Lucy had said about their baby. That there was something wrong.

'She hasn't ... yet. But I wouldn't put it past her.'

'No one knows about any of this?'

'No. So you'll understand why I'm not all that concerned about her situation. If she's pulled the same stunt with anyone else...'

My brain was reeling trying to re-assemble the picture of what had been going on.

'Do you think that's possible?'

'I don't know. Look, I know she's had a hard time of things ... I don't know how much she's told you.'

'Some,' I said not wanting to betray any confidences.

'Well, heavy stuff. You wouldn't believe one person could take all that. Maybe that's why she's like she is.'

'Perhaps she misunderstood the signals,' I

tried. 'It happens.'

'No,' he gave a thin smile. 'I never gave her any hint that I was interested. Nothing. I went out of my way to avoid her as soon as I realised what her game was. She kept on, popping up here there and everywhere, talking as though there was something between us. Pretending intimacy. So I gave it to her straight.' He gave a little laugh of disbelief. 'That's when she threatened to ring my wife. I asked her not to. "Depends on you," she said, "perhaps the two of us need to get away together, have some time with each other." Fantasies.' I saw the anguish in his face, the torment that lay beneath the anger.

'You could explain to your wife yourself?'

It was hardly my place to be suggesting strategies against my client but if Lucy Barker had threatened him as he claimed and he really was the innocent party then telling his wife would take away the weapon of blackmail she was wielding.

'She's under a lot of stress, it's not a good time.'

A buzzer sounded and he bent over his desk. Rhona's voice sounded reedy through the connection. 'Call for you, Harry Clayton.'

'I need to take this,' Ian Hoyle said.

I nodded, thanked him and left him to get on with it.

Coming away there was a feeling of outrage lodged just below my breastbone. Lucy Barker had been lying to me. Whatever the truth was about her relationship with Ian Hoyle, she had invented her account of seeing him and checking him out. It must have been a ploy to stop me talking to him. She'd been adamant that I shouldn't interview him again. But I'd gone behind her back and now I had some serious talking to do with Miss Barker.

Trying her mobile and even her home number I only got the messaging services. A long weekend and I'd no idea where she'd gone. She knew that I might try and ring if anything arose. What if she was in trouble? After an hour or so I started to worry. I was furious at her deception but she was still my client. I drove over to her house in Levenshulme. Her car, a green Mondeo, wasn't there which reassured me a bit and there was no answer when I rang her bell. There was no sign of anything wrong.

I salvaged the rest of the afternoon by skiving off work and catching up with the gardening. The house boasts a good-sized plot; well, good for the city, and there's space for borders and a play area as well as a patio, lawn and shed. I'm the only one who ever does any gardening though now and then Ray will build me something that I need, like a cold frame or a trellis arch. It was bitter out there, the cold snap had started and it made my nose run incessantly as I spread horse manure over the beds and pulled out the first eager weeds. The daffodils were over and I tied up their leaves into little top knots; they looked ridiculous but apparently if I didn't the things would weaken and fail to flower. A wren with its distinctive small, dumpy shape and sharply angled tail was hopping about in a shrub at the bottom of the garden. I'd not seen it in previous years and I wondered whether it was nesting nearby. I was familiar though with the robin which came and watched me whenever I got the spade out: wise to the prospect of a worm or two.

Gradually my frustration with the case eased. There was nothing I could do till Lucy Barker contacted me. I'd asked her to tell me where she was. Would she? And would she check her messages, or would that ruin her weekend? My weekend was mapped out. Friday night I'd do self defence. I also needed to have a good chat with Maddie plus I'd promised her a trip to the pictures. It was Chris's party at the Irish Club on Saturday night and somewhere along the line I needed to fit in my final night observation at Severn Road. There was a gust of wind and my eyes watered. God, it was cold. I thought of Mrs Smith in the decaying house, no socks, probably precious little heating. How would she and her husband keep warm? Climb into bed? Sit swaddled in newspapers? I shivered. Time to clear up. And grab a hot drink. There were plenty of other things to occupy me, I would put Lucy Barker on hold until she crawled back out of the woodwork. And with that thought I realised how much my attitude towards my client had shifted.

Chapter Eleven

A new term at my Friday night self-defence class meant new faces. Ursula, our instructor, took this as a welcome opportunity to go right back to basics with us all. She took us through her ABC – alert, balanced, considered – illustrating her philosophy that our aim was to get out of any threatening situation without getting physical if at all possible. D (defuse) and E (escape) were better than F (fight).

The class was a mixed bunch. Some, like me, went because their work exposed them to risks. My sparring partner Brian was the same, he'd set up his own security business, offering door staff to clubs or parties and protection to people at risk who were worried and wealthy enough to shell out for his presence.

Other people came for a variety of reasons: they'd been on the receiving end of violence and wanted to prevent it happening again; they wanted a physical discipline that would develop their confidence; they saw it as a way to keep fit; or they'd seen a Bruce Lee film but wanted something without the martial arts trappings.

The old church hall we used was cold and echoey. As Ursula demonstrated the differing effects body language can have in a confrontation I thought about the woman who'd been attacked near Severn Road. Had she been out on her own since? Out in the dark? Was she recovering well or was she still traumatised, fearful of strangers and of her own dreams?

I knew from bitter experience how deep the scars could go. Coming to the classes was my insurance policy. And, after getting hurt before, I had promised Ray and my friend Diane that I'd make sure I was better equipped to protect myself in future.

Brian and I took turns to play the aggressor and to practise some of the techniques for calming the situation down. Tone of voice was important, eye contact or avoiding it, stance and so on. Lucy Barker kept disrupting my concentration. How was I going to tackle her? Why had she pretended to me that she'd talked to Ian Hoyle? Because she didn't want me to hear his version of events which made her out to be the spurned party? A matter of pride? Foolish to be bothered about that when she was being threatened with more serious harm. And who did I believe?

I called in home afterwards and sorted out my supplies for my final stint at Severn Road for the Ecclestones. It was very cold and if I used the car heater I'd drain the battery. So I filled two hot water bottles, packed a space blanket to sit on and a nifty foot warmer that had caught my attention in one of those gadget catalogues. It was filled with gel and once heated up it stayed warm for hours. Hot soup in a flask, a couple of rolls of bread and a large chocolate bar completed my preparations.

When I parked up, just before eleven, the street was deserted. On Friday night the optimum time for any bother would be from closing time onwards. Manchester now boasted it was a 24-hour city. Bit of an exaggeration: there is an all-night super-market somewhere but even that shuts at five on a Sunday. A handful of late bars and clubs run till five in the morning, but I compromised. I'd sit it out until three when the majority of places would have shut. Time stretched before me like a life sentence. I told myself to think of the money. After forty minutes I drove the length of the road and round the block, slowing as I passed the house where I'd dropped off the injured woman. The stained glass panel in the door glowed red and green from the light in the hall but there was no clue as to whether anyone was home.

By half-past eleven the first trickle of people began to return home on foot and I assumed most had been out drinking locally. I made another circuit to check whether anything was kicking off at the far end of the road but all seemed quiet. An hour or so later, with soup and rolls gone, I was startled by sudden loud noise, shouting and screeching. A gang of teenage girls came into view in my rear mirror. They were making a right racket. I found myself tensing up, my spine tightening as I imagined them noticing me, deciding to have some fun. One of them was copiously sick at the corner and the others reacted with a mix of hilarity and revulsion. Then they began to sing off-key and very loudly: *Let Me Entertain You.*

They teetered past on the opposite side of the road and stopped to light cigarettes. None of them even looked my way. With bare midriffs and exposed shoulders they were oblivious to the cold even though frost was visible, glistening on the pavement and the garden walls. It was a good job I'd resisted the temptation to buy a load of bedding plants over the Easter break. I'd have lost half of them.

At two I put my audio-book on to stop myself falling asleep. I kept the volume low and easily heard an alarm bell start up, cutting through the night air. I switched the cassette player off and tried to work out where the whooping was coming from. I drove down Severn Road and towards the flashing light that came into view near the end of the street. An old silver Nissan roared past me, young men in the front wearing baseball hats. Coincidence? Or had the alarm sent them on their way?

Lights came on inside the house where the box was flashing and a few moments later the awful din stopped. A huge man in a dressing gown peered out of the front door, scowled at me for a while and then went inside again. None of his neighbours in the terraced row made an appearance. Another attempted burglary or just a false alarm?

I drove back round the block but this time I parked lower down Severn Road opposite the ramshackle Smith house. Hard to believe that anyone lived there, it had such an air of abandoned neglect. An owl cried, loud and close by. The overgrown garden would be good hunting ground.

The place became very quiet then. A stillness hung in the air. It began to snow. Large, soft flakes hit the windscreen and melted slightly then they came down thickly. I shivered. Two forty-five a.m. The heat was almost gone from my hotties and my toes. I was weary and wanted to go home. What had I found out for the Ecclestones? One false alarm and a few high-spirited clubbers to add to the report: neither a crime wave nor idyllic seclusion. Would the dispirited feeling I had have been different if the place had been a hot-bed of car stealing and street fighting? You do your job, I muttered to myself, you gets your money.

I drove carefully leaving fresh tracks on the white roads. I saw no one. The sense of being the only person awake reminded me of the nights when Maddie was a baby and I would sit and feed her and look out at a deserted city. Now and then I would hear the shriek of brakes from a night bus on Wilmslow Road and just before dawn the clatter and hum of the milk float going by.

Saturday morning. I tried Lucy Barker's numbers again and left more messages. Please ring and let me know that everything is all right.

The frosting of snow drew the kids into the garden like a magnet. There wasn't enough to make a snowman but they scraped together a few snowballs and ran around. They came in not long after, peeling sodden gloves off to reveal bright pink fingers.

After breakfast I got on with the chores: washing, drying, cleaning, tidying. When Ray took Tom off to visit his grandma, Nana Tello, I suggested to Maddie that she get her pens out and do some drawing.

'With you?'

I hadn't meant that but if it made her happy.

We messed about doing snowmen and elves and goblins. Neither of us were much cop. She seemed quite relaxed until I told her I wanted to talk about the problems at school. Her face shuttered, she stopped colouring in.

'I'm not going to tell you off or anything,' I said, 'I want you to tell me your side of things.'

She said nothing. Her mouth tightened in a little line, her fingers rolled the coloured pencil round and round.

'It's not like you to pick on somebody, to call people names. Is that really what happened?'

Mute.

'Why did you pick on Carmel?'

A flush of guilt softened her face and my stomach lurched in sympathy. She still avoided looking at me and didn't answer.

'Maddie, you know I love you.'

She frowned, dug her pencil into the paper and began scribbling, a blot of colour, a spiral of red, round and round.

'I want you to be happy, I want to help but it's hard if you won't talk to me.'

She shot me a black look and returned to her paper this time scribbling zigzag lines over the characters she'd drawn. Obliterating them. I reached out and put my hand on hers. 'Come here,' I said.

Reluctantly she sidled round to me. I pulled her onto my knee, put my arms around her. She didn't yield. I'd been hoping for tears, a tantrum, anything to release her from this stiff withdrawal.

With mounting exasperation I cast about for another opening. 'Is there anyone else you could talk to? Like Sheila?' Maddie had a mutual appreciation society going with our lodger. 'Or Ray?'

She gave a quick shake of her head.

'Has Carmel done anything to you?'

No response.

My temper rose but I resisted the urge to shake her or shout. 'When something horrible happens it feels better if you tell someone about it. If I'm upset or I've done something and wish I hadn't, I talk to Diane or Ray.'

She gave a little breathy sigh, swung her foot with impatience.

'Well,' I ground to a halt, 'you can always tell me about it some other time. And next week at school will be like a new start. Okay?'

She slid off my knee and left the room. I thumped the table and swore. Craving a coffee, I put the kettle on and got out the high roast. You couldn't force a child to talk but my attempt had gone down like a lead balloon. I was stumped.

After my coffee I sought Maddie out. She was lying on the floor in the lounge watching television. 'We could go to the park,' I suggested. 'See if the pond's frozen?'

She shook her head. 'It's too cold.'

'Okay,' I said firmly. 'You help me clear the playroom up after lunch.'

So we did. Sorting plastic, reuniting games and jigsaws. I tried to chuck away all the broken things that we'd never mend like legless dolls and a yoyo without a string while Maddie tried to stop me. 'You can't throw that away,' she'd say, 'that's my favourite.'

'You don't play with this anymore do you?' I gestured to the play cooker that took up a lot of space in one corner of the room.

'We do – sometimes.'

'We could put it in the cellar and just get it out when you want it.'

The cellar was an important strategic feature, a halfway house or handy staging post for items that would never come back upstairs but would move on from there to the next school fair, to other friends with younger children or to the bin.

After I'd carted it downstairs I saw it would make sense to rearrange the rest of the playroom. With Maddie's help I shifted dressing up clothes and books, moved the worktop on trestles which they used for crafts and games to beneath the bay window.

'It really needs a lick of paint,' I said. It was years since we'd decorated and the pale yellow walls were splattered with blu-tac craters, sellotape marks, felt pen scribbles, fragments of stickers, and here and there in indelible red ink and small, poorly formed letters, the word 'bum' – Tom's first graffiti.

'We could do a makeover,' Maddie beamed.

'Yes,' I tried not to think about the effort involved.

'Like *Changing Rooms*,' she referred to the

television DIY show.

'We'd have to agree on a colour, Tom as well.'

'I like purple.'

'It can look a bit dark.'

'Bright purple.'

'We'll look at some brochures.'

'Have you got some?'

'Somewhere, probably in the cellar.'

'Can we do new curtains?'

'I think we'll have to.' The ones at the window had come with the house. They were brown velvet now bleached an uneven caramel by the sun and with several small tears and holes in them.

It was good to see her excited about something. I had a root around in the cellar but I couldn't find any colour charts so we went off to B&Q and came back with a stack. Tom and Ray were back by then.

Before the two children had the chance to get into an argument about interior design I told them each to put a tick next to any colours they liked on the brochures and that we'd look at their ideas the following day. And we couldn't do stencils, I told them, pretending they were expensive. There was sound reasoning behind my embargo – one of the paint ranges was aimed at kids and I knew that Tom would fall for the action adventure design with its stencils of planes just as sure as Maddie would clamour for the underwater world with mermaids and fishes.

Chapter Twelve

Laura, Ray's girlfriend, joined us for tea. Ray made two lasagnes, one meat, one veggie and I got the lion's share of the latter.

'Whose party is it?' Laura asked me. They were babysitting that night.

'Chris, she used to live here.'

'When they were very small,' Ray nodded at the kids.

'She and her partner Jo bought a house in Hebden Bridge.'

'Very trendy,' said Laura.

'Yeah. They like it. I wouldn't fancy travelling into Manchester to work every day though. Chris is in the Housing Department.'

'Not a bad train service,' said Ray.

'When it's running. It's her fortieth,' I explained to Laura. 'Diane's done a picture for her, from the both of us.'

It was ages since I'd been to a party and I was looking forward to having a bit of a bop and seeing old friends. I wasn't dating anyone but there wasn't likely to be any talent at the party. There never was.

My party gear consisted of silky green trousers and a long jade green tunic with a mandarin collar. If I got too hot I could shed the tunic, I'd a black vest top underneath shot through with glitter.

'You look nice,' Maddie came in, already in her pyjamas.

'Thank you.' I did a twirl then sat down to finish my make-up.

'Tom wants red.'

'Red?'

'For the playroom. Man U.'

'If we got the shades right we could do red and purple. It would look very ... loud.'

'I think it'd be yucky.'

'We'll see what you've picked tomorrow. You go to bed now, I'll come and say night-night in a little while.'

When I looked in on her she was already asleep. Tom had kicked his covers off so I put them back.

Even with the central heating on their room was cool. The weather forecast predicted that freezing temperatures would continue until mid-week. And previous years were quoted when freak conditions had given us a Siberian spring.

I heard the taxi hoot outside and climbed in the back beside Diane, my larger-than-life friend. She'd got a parka style coat on with a fun fur trim on the hood. With her bulk it made her look like a Yeti. The heater was full on in the cab and I pulled off my own hat and gloves.

'Aren't you hot?'

'Don't laugh,' she said very slowly and clearly. 'Or scream.' She pushed back her hood.

'Bloody hell, Diane!'

I could see her skull, nearly all of it. There were three stripes of hair dyed a silvery colour, running front to back. Like an albino skunk.

'You don't like it,' she accused me.

'Since when did you care whether I liked it or not?' Messing about with her hair was Diane's hobby: striking cuts, blatant colours but she'd never had anything this ... brutal. And she'd never expressed doubts before.

'I've got a wig,' she thrust her hand into her pocket and drew out a swathe of straight honey coloured nylon hair.

I shrugged.

She pulled it on her head. She still looked weird but not so extreme.

'Try it off again?'

She complied then grumbled. 'The other thing is it's bloody freezing. If I'd known we were suddenly going to go sub-Arctic I might have gone for something else.'

My eyes betrayed me – she spotted the glimmer.

'Pack it in,' she shoved me.

'I'm sorry,' I giggled. 'It's good to laugh.'

'Not when it's at me.

'Reduces stress.'

'For you maybe.' She pulled the blonde wig firmly back into place.

'It'll grow.'

'I know. I don't often get it wrong,' she said slowly.

'There was that perm...'

'Sal,' she warned.

'Okay.'

We paid off the taxi outside The Irish Club and made our way to the upstairs function room. The party was well underway. Chris had booked a disco: two blokes who played a good mix of music, not run of the mill stuff but plenty of Tamla and funk, dance music, disco and lots of Latin. Chris and Jo had been going to Salsa classes for ages and, judging by the gymnastics on the dance floor, so had some of the other guests.

Diane and I queued up to give our present to Chris, who already looked very merry. Jo at her side gave us a wink. She knew about the gift because Diane had talked to her about what colour-scheme would work best in their house. She also raised her eyebrows at Diane's new look.

Chris stood up and gave each of us a hug and a kiss on the cheek. Diane hefted the large rectangular parcel up. Chris's eyes widened. There wasn't room to lay it flat on the table littered with drinks and gifts.

'Here,' Diane ushered her to one end of the buffet tables where there was more space and Chris unwrapped it.

'Oh, Diane it's beautiful, absolutely. It's perfect.'

'From us both,' Diane said.

'It's wonderful.'

I agreed. The print Diane had done was based on a photograph of their house and the hills in the background. I didn't know all the ins and outs of how she'd done it but the end result was like a cross between a primitive painting and an etching. It reminded me a bit of the wax crayon picture kids do at school where they build up layers of colour on black paper and then scratch away lines to reveal a drawing with a variety of colours. Chris hugged her again and dragged us off to meet her parents and some of her brothers and sisters, most of whom had travelled up from Wales for the party.

I went and queued for a drink while Diane circulated. The bar was busy but I got chatting to Rachel who hadn't found out anything in social services about the status of the Smiths yet. When I got served I took the drinks over to the edge of the dance floor where Diane had found seats.

After a couple of drinks Diane and I were ready to strut our stuff. I'd forgotten how good it was to dance and stayed up until I was breathless and I'd shed my tunic. Diane must have been boiling in the wig. She went off for more drinks and I sat getting my breath back when a new group of people arrived. Four women. My stomach tumbled as I recognised one of them. Blonde hair, small frame, the woman who'd sat in my car, crying, with her nose bleeding, shaking with fear.

They were across the room from me by the bar, talking to Chris. Dancers kept blocking my view. Was it really her?

When Diane came back I asked her if she knew any of them. She ducked a bit to see and shook her head. 'Why?'

Usually I confide in Diane about work as well as everything else. I trust her but it didn't feel right to explain at that point.

'One of them looks familiar,' I said.

I was unsettled. Without making it obvious I was alert to every move the woman made, anxious to confirm it was her and uneasy that she had turned up here. A nasty part of my work had suddenly spilled into my social life. If it was the woman I also wanted to know whether she'd changed her mind about reporting the attack.

The music was loud and it was hard to talk at any length, though I gave Diane a brief run down of the problems with Maddie. The group of women organised seats close to the bar. Eventually my curiosity drove me over there. I stopped nearby to have a word with Chris and kept one eye on the woman I was interested in. She was talking with her friends; when she glanced sideways and saw me she turned swiftly back. That reaction was all the confirmation I needed. I asked Chris about the group. She was very drunk by now.

'Friends from the Town Hall. Betty and Cleo, Caroline in the orange...'

'The woman next to Caroline?'

'Minty, her partner. Their place isn't far from you. I'll introduce you...'

I was saved a reply when Jo grabbed her arm and insisted they take the floor for Abba's 'Dancing Queen'.

I looked back to Minty. What should I say? She chose that moment to get up and set off to the far end of the room where the toilets were. I followed.

She was waiting by the sinks. There was no one else around.

'How are you?' In the stark fluorescent light I could see she was wearing a lot of make-up and had chosen violet eye shadow. Any bruises were well hidden.

'Don't say anything, please.' Her eyes flicked to the door and back. 'I just want to forget about it.'

'You haven't told your friends?'

A spike of panic flared in her eyes. She shook her head once.

'Your partner?' I said in disbelief. Surely she'd have had to tell her, to explain the state she was in.

'Of course I told her,' she amended. 'She wanted me to report him, like you. But I

160

can't, I can't face it. Please don't make it any worse.'

The door swung open as someone came in and she took the opportunity to walk out.

I felt horribly sober.

I hid it well, went back out and circulated, nattered to people I hadn't seen for years. Didn't dance anymore though. I watched Caroline and Minty dancing towards the end of the evening. They looked very happy. What about the man, would he attack again? Had he already? Would his crimes escalate? More savage beatings, rape, murder? How long until someone finally took the terrifying step of reporting him? Because I knew, just like everyone else, how vicious the justice system could be, even for witnesses – let alone victims. Let it be, I told myself, but there was a sour taste to the evening now and I never regained my party spirit.

Chapter Thirteen

There was a new Wallace and Gromit movie on at the cinema. I rang Katy's mum to check that Katy could come and arranged to pick her up on the way.

After a lazy breakfast I sat down with Maddie and Tom to look at colour charts. It was easier than I had expected. They had both ticked a vibrant turquoise. With white gloss, plain wood skirting boards and door and something light for the curtains it would look fine. The room was big enough to take the intense colour and there was even a dash of turquoise in the large rug.

'Can we paint it now?' Tom said.

'No, we've got to empty everything out first, cover the floor with dustsheets and get ladders for the ceiling. And buy the paint. First of all we need to move some of this.'

They helped for all of ten minutes but were regularly waylaid by finding toys that they'd forgotten about. The air was thick with nostalgia.

I moved boxes into the hallway and some

to the cellar. I'd done about half of it by lunchtime. Ray and Laura were just making brunch and Ray did fried egg sandwiches for me and the kids.

'Pictures this afternoon,' I announced. 'We're taking Katy.'

'What to see?' Tom asked.

'Wallace and Gromit.'

'Yes!'

Maddie's face hardened. 'I don't want to go.'

'Why not?'

'It's stupid.'

'It's the new one, it's supposed to be really good.'

'I don't want to go,' she yelled and stormed out.

Damn!

Laura and Ray exchanged glances.

'She's driving me nuts,' I said.

'Remember the penguin,' Tom supplied, harking back to one of the earlier films. 'That was wicked. His eyes went...' he narrowed his eyes, shifted them from side to side.

I finished my sandwich and went to find her. 'Why don't you want to go? And I want a proper reason.'

'Got a headache.'

'We're meant to be picking Katy up in half-an-hour. She'll be disappointed.'

'You could go,' she said in a small voice. 'I could stay with Ray.'

'But I wanted to go with you, I thought we'd have a really nice time.' I could hardly drag her kicking and screaming into the multiplex. I tried bribery. 'We can get popcorn and Coke, go for pizza after.'

She looked desolate.

When I explained the situation to Ray he offered to take Tom and I'd see if Katy wanted to go with them.

'She's got a headache,' I told Katy's mum, 'but it only came on after the pictures was mentioned.'

Katy didn't want to go without Maddie. I apologised again.

The rest of the day was low key. Maddie was subdued. I gave her Calpol for the headache and I carried on clearing the play room and made a nut-roast with all the trimmings for tea. It was still bitterly cold and a big meal seemed appropriate. We'd just finished eating when the phone rang.

'Sal, it's Lucy Barker.'

About time and all. I felt a rush of annoyance. 'Where are you?' I could hear the cool edge of my words.

'At home,' her voice was strained. 'Please, can you come?'

'Well, it's not...' I was about to put her off till the following day but then she blurted out. 'They've been here. Oh, please come,' and began to cry.

My stomach fluttered. 'All right, I'll be there as soon as I can.' Part of me was cursing her, still annoyed by the lies she'd spun me about Ian Hoyle but I was anxious too. Last time there had been dog muck, a death threat, malicious wounding and now...?

'How long will you be?' Ray asked.

'An hour, maybe a bit more.'

'We're going out.'

'Hell, when?'

'Starts at eight. Play at the Green Room, told you last week.'

'I remember, sorry. Sheila in?'

I went up to the top floor and knocked on Sheila's door. She was at her desk surrounded by papers, her glasses pushed up on top of her grey hair.

'Are you out tonight?'

'No,' she nodded at her work. 'Here for the duration.'

'Ray's off to the theatre and I've got to see a client – could you listen for Tom and

Maddie if I'm not back in time?'

'Of course I will.'

After a quick goodnight to Maddie I gathered hat, scarf, gloves and coat and set out. The car didn't like the cold and wouldn't start at first. I began to get panicky about it and yelped with relief when it finally caught.

The roads were quiet, I was in Levenshulme in ten minutes. I rang the front door bell and Lucy buzzed me in. She was at her flat door, she looked frightened: her eyes appeared larger and her complexion more pallid even though she still wore make-up.

She opened her mouth but words failed her, she shook her head, raised her hand and moved it, a gesture that said she was lost, didn't know where to begin. She took a step inside and I went after her. The place had been trashed, furniture was overturned, drawers emptied out, the chemical smell of acetone was heavy in the air.

DIE BITCH was scrawled across the wallpaper in red aerosol car-spray paint, the letters were uneven and rivulets of paint ran down like dripping blood.

I turned to her.

'Anywhere else?'

She turned without speaking and led me

into the kitchen. The floor was awash with spilt food, broken glass. Pools of sauce, sugar and rice, yoghurt.

'And here,' she spoke.

I hadn't been in her bedroom before. Again it had that peculiar mismatched look, the interior design so at odds with Lucy's own elegant style, with fleurs-de-lys stencils on rag-rolled ochre walls and ugly melamine furniture. I only thought about that later. At the time my attention was fixed on the bed. The covers had been stripped back, a knife was sticking out of a pool of red, the handle like a dagger, made of ivory or bone. Not subtle.

'Jesus,' I said softly. 'How'd they get in?'

'Kitchen window, smashed it.' Her face creased up.

'What about the alarm?'

She shook her head, bewildered.

I pulled out my phone and began to dial.

'Who are you ringing?'

'The police.'

'No!' she cried. 'No, you can't!'

'I can.'

'No!'

I cut the call.

'Look,' I was practically shouting at her. 'I'm not going to stand by and watch while things get even worse.' I pointed to the bed. 'That's no joke. What do you think they'll do next? What if you'd been here?'

She flinched and looked away.

'I'm getting nowhere but the police...'

'No.'

'For God's sake,' I wanted to throttle her. How could she be so dense? 'Whoever did this is dangerous. We have to report it. There's no alternative.' I made to dial again.

'No.'

'If you won't, I will.'

'Please no!'

I held up my hand to silence her, pressed the keypad.

'Don't!' She yelled. 'I know who did it. It was Benjamin!'

'What?'

'Benjamin,' she repeated.

Oh, great. Now she'd really flipped. The ghost of her dead fiancé was to blame. Of course.

'Lucy, he's dead.'

'That's his knife.' Her voice caught. She turned and walked back into the lounge forcing me to follow. She stood in the window pressing her palms together nervously.

'He's dead,' I repeated.

'He isn't,' she said and her eyes glimmered.

'The car crash.'

She shook her head.

'But–'

She batted her hands together fast and light.

'Lucy?'

She ducked her head, glanced at me then away, looked at a spot near the skirting board in the corner of the room. 'He walked away from it,' she spoke with effort, as though the words were the wrong shape in her mouth. 'He left me there.' She paused. In the quiet I heard the rumble of a plane coming into the airport. 'He was sick.'

'Sick? How?'

'They don't know exactly. Out of control, impulsive. He wasn't safe.' Pain burned bright in her eyes making her frown.

'How do you mean?'

She took a quick breath. 'Benjamin was very jealous. I had to be very careful. After the accident he got much worse. Some sort of brainstorm. He needed treatment.'

'Wait, I don't understand. Tell me again.'

'Benjamin is very ... possessive. He was driving like a maniac when we had the accident.'

She paused.

'You said he left you there?'

'They think he was concussed. He said he couldn't remember any of it. Then his behaviour got very erratic, sort of a breakdown. He needed psychiatric treatment.'

'When was this?'

'Fifteen months ago. I moved here once I'd finished physio.'

'Your engagement?'

Her fingers sought out the ring. 'I said I'd wait – till he was better.'

'And you think this ... you think he–?'

She nodded, tears splashed from her eyes.

'Oh, God.' I righted a chair and sat down. 'But why?'

'When he's ill, he thinks I've betrayed him, somehow. Gets in a rage.'

I ran my hands over my face. 'Why on earth didn't you tell me?'

'I didn't know it was him. I didn't want to believe ... I hoped I was wrong.'

I felt the glow of anger spread as the ramifications of her secrecy struck home. 'You put us both at risk.' The lies about Ian Hoyle flashed into my mind. Small fry. I'd get to those later. 'Have you any idea...' I broke off, outrage snatching my words. 'Why didn't you tell me what you suspected?' I demanded.

'I didn't want it to be him. I didn't want to

think it. I love him.' She protested through her tears.

'So why bother getting me in at all?'

'I was scared. And I wasn't sure. I wanted you to prove it one way or another.'

'And if it was Benjamin?'

'I still love him.'

I stared at her, appalled. 'So what are you saying? If it's Benjamin do nothing?'

'No,' a small voice.

'Well, then?'

'I won't press charges, I won't have him arrested and...'

'You can't let him carry on.'

'Get him help,' she gulped.

I ran my hand through my hair, struggled to collect my thoughts. 'I can't believe you let me...' I exhaled. Tried again. 'But now you're sure. Because of the knife. Has he done this sort of thing before? Hate mail, threats?'

'Not exactly. Phone calls, before I moved.'

'This was after the accident?'

'Yes.'

'You say he had treatment.'

'He had to go into hospital.'

'And you were still seeing him?'

She scowled, fought back tears. 'I went to visit, he...' she sniffed, '...he thought I was

being unfaithful, he tried to–' One hand
went to her neck. I got the idea.

'He attacked you?'

She nodded. 'They said it was best to give
him time. He used to phone.'

'And threaten you?'

'I moved. But I promised to wait. To
marry him when he was well again.'

'And since then?'

'I got a Christmas card. He was fine. Out
of hospital, working again. He still needed
time but he said how much it meant,
knowing I'd stand by him, that when he was
ready I'd be here.'

And she'd gone round telling people he
was dead. Why not just ditch the ring and
not mention him? Was she simply a habitual
liar? One of those people for whom the
truth is never quite enough.

'So all this?'

'He must have got worse again. He needs
help.'

'Where's he living?'

'I don't know.'

'What about work?'

'He's a doctor.'

'A doctor!' I don't know why I was so
surprised. As if doctors don't go off the rails
like the rest of us. 'GP?'

'Hospital. He was.'

'But you don't know where?'

'He didn't say.'

'Where was he before?'

'Leicester. We both were.'

I took a couple of breaths tried to steady my pulse rate. Now what?

'I could write to him,' she said, 'if I had an address.'

'What?'

'Reassure him, tell him to go see someone. He'll listen to me.'

She was barking.

'Lucy, the guy has just broken in, smashed up your home, stuck a knife in your bed.'

'You don't understand,' she dismissed me. 'Last time it was me who persuaded him to get help. He trusts me.'

More than I bloody do.

'Look, don't come back here on your own. Get anything you need and stay at the B&B for now.'

'Benjamin–'

I cut her off. 'I need to think.'

'I won't go to the police.' Her tone was cold, emphatic. She no longer patted her hands together.

'Are you working tomorrow?'

'Yes.'

'I'll warn Malcolm.'

'But–'

'He needs to know, Lucy. He can keep an eye on you. Keep a look out for Benjamin.'

'I don't think Benjamin would–'

'A precaution. This place has been the target so far but I don't want to take any risks. I need a photograph.'

Her eyes roved to the gallery she had by her flat door. She grimaced but went over and took one down, in a clip-frame, and gave it to me. I looked briefly at the picture, the young man had dark hair, a longish face, slightly protruding upper jaw, glasses. Nothing remarkable. And I didn't think I'd seen anyone like that hanging around in the previous days.

I asked her a couple more questions; Benjamin's surname, Vernay, and his date of birth which she supplied.

'I'll meet you at lunchtime. We'll talk about it then.' And the rest. I couldn't think clearly anymore. It was as if she'd got a stick and muddied my mind up.

En route to the B&B I checked to see whether any vehicle followed us but none did. I left her getting her room key. She'd regained her composure and as she spoke with the woman who ran the guest house nothing betrayed the upheaval of the last few hours. I couldn't help but admire the control she had, the nerve. Though I found it hard to stomach her loyalty to the man who was persecuting her.

Chapter Fourteen

I'd had quite a weekend of it what with running into Minty at the party, Maddie's refusal to talk and now this truckload of revelations from Lucy Barker. At least the house assessment for the Ecclestones had been fairly straightforward. My report would be a warts and all look at the area. They'd have to weigh up whether the level of petty crime was acceptable given how much they liked the house. As a financial move they couldn't really lose out.

Maddie had another headache on Monday morning. I wasn't surprised. She was probably dreading school but I thought it was crucial that she go in and start her new regime. If she could get though the week and gain positive points it would be an achievement to build on and things would hopefully seem that much brighter. Keeping her at home would signal failure at the outset. I told her she had to go to school and that I was sure she'd do really well. We could start on painting the playroom after tea. She looked mildly interested. At school I waited with her in the classroom, not something I'd done since she moved up to Juniors. She let me kiss her when I left. I tried not to let it worry me.

I faxed the Ecclestones their report as agreed and closed their file. Always a satisfying moment. As I prepared for my meeting with Lucy Barker I was still stuck in a tape loop of incredulity. With each fresh incident that came to mind: knocking on her flatmates' doors, meeting Carly Jowett, interviewing hotel staff, another bout of disbelief washed over me – how could she let me do all that when she'd known, from the word go? Didn't she feel at all uncomfortable as I went through the motions, doing my best to find the culprit? Had she got some sort of sick thrill out of watching me flail about?

I could have walked away right then. I was tempted. It would have been justified. But I hate to leave things unfinished. After being mucked about I wanted some resolution.

And it shouldn't involve much more of my time and energy – track down Dr Benjamin Vernay and deliver an ultimatum: the harassment stops immediately or the law will be involved. Lucy might resist it but that was my bottom line. Of course she could also send whatever *billets doux* or letters of support she liked but my terms were non-negotiable. If he so much as made a silent phone call I'd report him even if Lucy wouldn't. Of course there was the odd kink I hadn't quite ironed out – Lucy might not tell me if he did resume his nasty tricks – but I didn't dwell on that.

There was another reason for not wanting to quit: if I didn't see it through and warn off Vernay and then something happened to Lucy I'd feel responsible. Call it an honourable exit. I'd do my best and then say goodbye with an easy conscience and an immense sense of relief. The theory was fine; the reality was an absolute nightmare.

Hoping that Malcolm, the hotel security manager, would help protect Lucy, I made a copy of Benjamin Vernay's photo to give him. Lucy was already in reception when I arrived, a bright red manikin in the luminous white of the foyer. Her practised smile became frostier when I asked to see

Malcolm. She still didn't like the idea that darling Benjamin might pose a threat.

Malcolm Whitlow greeted me with something akin to disapproval when he came to the foyer. I didn't blame him; the last time I'd been there his boss had wanted me chucked out and had then done an about-face. I was troublesome. His amenable attitude and apparent acceptance of my work on our first meeting had evaporated. Malcolm had half a scowl on his face and sighed with ill concealed impatience as I asked for a few minutes of his time.

'It's about Lucy,' I told him glancing across to the desk where she was dealing with a group of Japanese guests. 'Is there somewhere more private?'

He humphed and took me along the ground floor corridor to his room.

'There's been a break-in at her flat but we know who's behind it now.' I proffered the picture. 'Dr Benjamin Vernay, her old fiancé.'

He narrowed his eyes, pursed his lips in a silent whistle and cast me a look of surprise.

'I know,' I said, 'she told everyone he was dead but he was sick.' He listened to a potted history. 'It's not very likely he'll come here,' I concluded, 'he's only been to the flat when Lucy's been out and he's been very careful not to be seen. But just in case...' I gestured to the picture.

He nodded. He waited till I was on my feet and about to leave before he commented. 'So she knew all along it was him?'

I gave a rueful sigh. 'Yep.'

He exhaled. He didn't speak, didn't need to. The downturn of his mouth, upward swoop of his eyebrows and the bald disapproval in his eyes summed up perfectly how bloody daft he thought that was. I didn't disagree.

Lucy was waiting for me at reception. I thought we'd be having a bite to eat but she told me she'd been ill and couldn't face anything. 'I had internal bleeding – after the accident. It flares up with the stress,' she explained.

He walked away, he left me there.

'We can walk?' I offered.

She went to get her coat. I surveyed one of the huge stone sculptures, a wedge of white limestone, the layers visible in the rock like sheets of pastry. I ran my hand along the cold, hard edge. The limestone formed from the shells and skeletons of sea-creatures over millions of years. Forged into the hills of the Peak District south of Manchester and the Yorkshire Dales over the Pennines. I wondered where they had got the piece from. Imagined someone having a job that involved selecting rocks for customers.

Lucy returned buttoned into a long, warm, camel classic. We set off towards the canal.

'The accident – what happened exactly? You said Benjamin was driving dangerously?'

She glanced at me, looked away.

'He was angry. We'd been to the theatre with friends, another doctor and his wife. Benjamin thought I'd been making eyes at the man. He was mad at me. I was trying to calm him down but he took a bend too fast, an old country lane, there was a wall ... we hit it head on. It took them hours to cut me free.'

'And Benjamin?'

'He got out.'

'You said he just left you there.'

'He was concussed, confused. This way.'

We took the footbridge, a span of bright white suspension rods and turrets reminiscent of lighthouses at either end, over the Ship Canal towards the Imperial War Museum North. The canal widened to a large basin on our left with marina apartments all along the far waterfront and the Designer Outlet complex at the near-side. To our right the great canal that had brought trade to Salford and Manchester in their industrial heyday flowed east towards the coast some forty miles away. We walked past the theatre ship, 'Walk The Plank', with its quirky murals and inventive artefacts, and along the quayside. It was windier there, a breeze riffling the earthen coloured water, stirred the surface into leaf-shaped ribbons that caught the blue of the sky. The light bounced off the metallic cladding of the War Museum. Everywhere bright and shiny, the vista wide, beneath the arc of the heavens.

'I've explained the situation to Malcolm,' I said. 'I think you should stay at the B&B until I've traced Benjamin and put everything in writing to him.'

She began to speak but I raised my hand. I wanted to say my piece.

'And that includes a clear warning: if there's any further harassment, letters, calls, anything we go straight to the police and tell them everything.'

'But–'

'It's not up for discussion,' I said firmly.

'I couldn't go to the police.'

'Well, I could.'

'I was raped, remember?'

Her first term at college, forced to report it, and how the treatment of the police had felt as pitiless as the attack itself. I blanched but stood my ground.

'I hope that this will be the end of it but if he carries on I'll report him with or without you.'

She looked at me bleakly. 'I don't have any choice.'

'No. To be frank I don't think a letter from you asking Benjamin to get help is going to make any difference but the clear threat of legal action might. You're entitled to protection,' I reminded her.

She shook her head, tight-lipped at my folly.

'One false step and we apply for an injunction.'

'We're getting married,' she cried.

'Really,' I said hotly, 'when? Does Benjamin know? You haven't seen him for months, he slashes your bed and sends you razor blades and dog-shit.'

'I won't desert him, I won't.' She became agitated, her fists tight little balls waving about as she spoke.

'That's up to you,' I said, 'but the only way

182

I'm prepared to deal with the guy is to read him the Riot Act. I'm not pussy-footing about. Once that's done and you feel ready to go home I'll get Brian to beef up your security. Your alarm needs sorting out, maybe even a new one.'

'I know. How will you trace him?'

'It shouldn't be that hard if he's still in the medical profession, Vernay's not a common name.'

A tug of wind made me shiver. I was hungry as well as cold.

'Head back?'

'How long will it take – to find him?'

'A day or two I hope.'

We walked back heading into the wind. It was cold enough to make my eyes water. Lucy wiped at hers with a tissue.

'There's something else,' I said. 'I know about Ian Hoyle.'

She frowned at me, sniffed. 'What do you mean?'

'Lucy, please,' I spoke sharply. 'Can't you just tell the truth? According to Ian, he wasn't chasing you – it was the other way around.'

'No.' She stopped walking and pulled at my arm. Her eyes were wide and steely. 'I would never...' She broke off as a couple approached us and smiled a little un-certainly. We must have looked like we were in the middle of a row. She turned back to me. 'I told you, there's no one else for me. How could you...' She was really riled, shaking and her nostrils flaring.

I took a slight step to the side just in case she lost it and tried to push me into the canal.

'I told you what happened, Ian was all mixed up, his wife, the baby...'

'I don't believe you.' I'd had enough of her games. 'I've talked to him. You never even went to see him on Wednesday but you spun me some line about him feeling sorry for you. More lies. Now I know why you were so sure it couldn't be Ian because you knew it was Benjamin all along. How can I trust you? You've been lying from day one.'

I waited for her response.

She looked at me, her face paled and she swayed. She put a hand to her stomach.

'Lucy?'

'Sorry,' she blurted out, she bent double and began to retch. Nothing came out. After a moment she stopped, straightened, her eyes and nose running.

'I'd like to go back.'

She looked awful. But how convenient,

too – a neat sidestep to avoid dealing with my accusations. Like Maddie's sudden tummy aches writ large.

There was an e-mail waiting from my journalist friend Harry; about the hate mail. Someone could do me a breakdown of the lettering and likely sources for six hundred pounds. Hollow laugh. No need now though, with Benjamin in the frame. But there was something else Harry could help me with. There are various ways to trace people, I use them myself: phone directories, the electoral roll, but they take time and they rely on someone being settled for a while. I wanted to find Dr Benjamin Vernay fast. One source of information growing by the minute is the electronic data kept on us all and updated every time we use a credit card. Ring up to renew your car insurance or order something mail order and they can access your details at the click of a mouse. The records are confidential, supposedly. It's murky territory and not something I'm experienced at. I asked Harry to do the deed for me.

'If you need to pay anyone a fee...'
'A favour,' he said. 'But you owe me.'
'Done.'

'Could be a day or two.'

I drafted a letter to the doctor, stating in no uncertain terms that a restraining order would be sought if Dr Benjamin Vernay came within spitting distance of Lucy Barker, her residence or place of work. Not my exact words. Unsolicited mail, phone-calls, e-mails, text messages and all other forms of communication of a threatening or abusive nature were also off-limits.

To pump it up a bit I added that incriminating evidence would be passed to the police if the above conditions were broken. I faxed a copy of the letter to a solicitor I know and asked her if there was anything I should change.

Not long, I thought, and I'd be rid of Lucy Barker and glad to see the back of her. By her own warped logic I'd done what she set out to get me to do – establish who was after her. If anything else happened it would be the police. My services do not include taking on jealous and demented knife-wielding boyfriends. I've a thing about knives as it is – they cut, they hurt, people die.

The school run. I still felt awkward in the playground but Katy's mum, Fiona, greeted me as normal and it seemed that word hadn't got round that Maddie had been bullying.

'Headache gone?'

'No, but I sent her in anyway. She's a bit unsettled at the moment. There's been some trouble between her and another girl.' I didn't elaborate. I couldn't bring myself to label Maddie as a bully. I still felt so ashamed and appalled by it all.

'Katy wants her to come to tea.'

'Great.' One of my fears had been about Maddie getting isolated, losing her friends as a result of the bullying. Invitations to tea were reassuring.

'Tomorrow – I'll pick her up from school?'

Tom came out then and shoved a pile of drawings and his lunch box at me.

'Can I go to Adam's house one day?'

He dragged me over to his friend and within minutes I'd fixed it so both Tom and Maddie would be out the following tea time.

When Maddie's class came out Miss Dent gave me a quick nod. All was well and Maddie seemed quite bright as we walked home; telling me about an experiment they'd done to see which materials were waterproof.

Ray cooked tea and I set to work in the

playroom, tacking dustsheets over the door, covering the skirting board and fixing big polythene sheets across the bay so the windows wouldn't get splattered turquoise.

Maddie and Tom donned old clothes. Ray steered clear. He's not averse to painting but he has a fastidious side so the prospect of gobs of emulsion flying about as the kids got stuck in was anathema to him. I used a tall stepladder to start on the ceiling while Maddie and Tom had a roller and a tray and a wall each. At the end of an hour I'd done a complete coat on the ceiling with fetching highlights on my hair, Tom had managed to tread in his tray and track paint everywhere and Maddie had done a two foot strip the length of her wall then given up because her arms ached. The turquoise was certainly a strong colour; it seemed to glow.

I called to Ray to run a bath while I cleared up. After the kids had been cleaned I got in the bath and rolled little curds of paint off my face and arms. Dry and dressed and with a sense of satisfaction we sat down to home-made potato wedges and sweetcorn, they had fried chicken and I had spinach and cream cheese sauce. References to snot and mould were made by the kids but my appetite was unaffected.

Later on, settled in the lounge, the kids asleep, I told Ray about plans for the following day.

'And how did Maddie get on?'

'Good.'

He stretched. Yawned. 'I went into TXL,' he said referring to his new computing job at the IT company, 'to talk about my hours.'

'And?'

'They've agreed to a three day week – long days but I can handle that. But they want me to do a month full-time first so they can train me alongside the rest of the intake.'

'Right, I can work round that. When do you start?'

'Week after next.'

'What about holidays?'

'Six weeks plus bank holidays. The summer will be tricky. There's always my mum.'

I shot him a look. 'For a morning here and there maybe.' Nana Tello, while protesting her adoration of 'il bambino' Tom, actually found the whole babysitting business quite hard work. Plus she had a lively social life and hated to miss out on seeing her friends. There was no way she'd do more than the odd emergency stretch.

'Let's think about it,' I said. 'The kids are off for what? Two weeks at Easter and

189

Christmas,' I counted on my fingers, 'six in summer, three half terms. That's thirteen weeks. A quarter of the year! How do we all cope?'

'You'd end up doing the lion's share especially in the holidays. I'll be getting a decent salary though – enough to pay...'

'Oh, no,' I groaned, 'that would feel really weird.'

'But if you can't take a job on because you've only two days at half-term or whatever...'

'No. Let's just see how it works out.'

He shrugged – if you think so.

'What's it like? Very swanky? Full of breathtaking views of our fair city, real coffee machines, innovative art-works, quirky people being brilliant?'

He laughed. 'If only. I've not met many of the people yet but the place is sectioned off into cubby-holes; it'll be like sitting in a wardrobe all day.'

'Least you can escape into virtual reality.'

'Only way to cope.'

My phone interrupted us. When I answered there was a moment's silence as though the caller was disconcerted to reach me, then she spoke, her voice low.

'Sal Kilkenny?'

'Yes?'

'It's Minty, from the party.'

As if I wouldn't remember her – and it wasn't the party I thought of but the way she'd stumbled past my car.

'I'm scared.' Her voice broke.

A chill crawled down my spine.

'Please...'

I couldn't tell whether she was pleading with me or someone else. I couldn't hear anything. Had she stopped speaking or was there a problem with the connection.

'Minty? Minty?' My phone displayed call ended. I pressed to re-dial but it switched to an answering service. Ray had been watching and had picked up on the concern in my voice.

'She's gone,' I said to him, 'said she was scared then broke off.'

'A client?'

'No. The woman I told you about from last week, the one who'd been mugged and I took her home. Turns out she knows Chris, she was at the party.' I thought about it. 'Could be a panic attack, I suppose. I think I better call round see if she's at home.'

'She might ring back,' he said. 'Maybe you should wait?'

191

I grimaced. Feeling jumpy, I didn't want to sit and wait. What if the man had come back, maybe he was at her house, what if the first attack he'd simply been disturbed and now he was back, perhaps the beating had been a prelude to rape. My mind swayed around overloaded with possibilities.

'Give her my mobile if she does. It'll only take a little while to drive round there.'

He smiled.

'What?'

'You,' he said affectionately, 'never say no.' He stopped smiling. 'If this bloke's there...'

'I'll call the police,' I promised him.

Chapter Fifteen

I'd lost my gloves. Stupid things hang around cluttering up the place for months and then, when the temperature falls, abracadabra – like a fiver up a magician's sleeve. My hands ached from the cold bite of the steering wheel and when I stopped at lights I rubbed them together to try and stop the pain.

I parked directly outside Minty's and left

the car door unlocked just in case I had to get away in a hurry. I pushed the bell which rang loud and clear inside. Peering in through the stained glass I couldn't discern any movement; no sound of footsteps or doors opening. I rang again, three long bursts, enough to wake the dead. The phrase disturbed me, I pushed away the thought – I was *not* prepared to think like that. One phone call from an anxious woman did not a murder make.

Still no one came. I was loathe to leave but what else could I do. Minty had rung me from a mobile, I didn't know her home number. I tried Chris but her answerphone was on.

I decided to check the back; her partner Caroline might be in there with the television on loud, though there was no noise audible from where I stood. Or the man who'd hurt Minty might have returned, got into the house and trapped her in one of the back rooms. The house was in a terrace and although these were bigger and more upmarket than most in Manchester they still shared alleyways that separated the row of back gardens from the gardens of the next street.

In the past, night soil carts and coal

wagons would have used the alleys, nowadays the residents dragged their wheelie bins along them once a week for the refuse collection. A solitary street lamp lit the passageway. I made my way along counting down to the fifth house. A lot of the windows were lit, paper blinds showed squares of cream, heavier curtains admitted only a strip of light around the edge, one upstairs room with curtains drawn framed the electric-blue flicker of a television set. Minty's back garden was fenced with larch-lap panels and a traditional wooden gate like a door. I tried the latch and it opened fine, the snick of noise rang loud in the cold, quiet air. I paused on the threshold, there was a faint glow at one of the upstairs windows but no lights visible in the downstairs rooms and from this distance no noise or sign of life. Should I go and peer in the windows?

I heard a sound, felt the movement of air and then the sudden crushing weight of an arm around my neck. He'd got me! Fear flashed along my limbs and slapped at my heart.

'What d'you think you're playing at?' His voice harsh in my ear.

Shock sizzled through my veins and I

fought for breath. I'd no image of the man who had hurt Minty but Benjamin Vernay's face sprang to mind. It couldn't be him, could it?

'Get off me,' I managed.

To my surprise he let go and I almost fell over. He was a large man, tall and broad with a tonsured head. He smelt of onions. He stared at me. My pulse was rocketing, my throat tightened. I couldn't remember my ABC from self-defence. I wanted to run and I wanted to hit the guy. I did neither. He was blocking the gate. Could he smell my fear? Did it give him a kick?

'Well,' he said, 'what do you think you're doing?'

It took me a moment to answer. How could we be talking like this when he was about to beat me up? Part of the game?

'I couldn't get a reply at the front, I thought I'd try here.'

He sneered. 'You were hanging about the other night,' he said.

My mouth was dry. He thought I'd seen the attack, thought I was a witness. He'd try to shut me up. I said nothing.

'Severn Road, I saw you then, so what do you do, eh? You the look-out? They didn't get in – your mates. I think the police would like to talk to you. I'm making a citizen's arrest. Oh, yes.' He gripped my upper arm. 'Bit of explaining to do, haven't you?'

'Wait!' It was the man I'd seen in his dressing gown on his front porch, the man whose alarm had gone off while I'd been working for the Ecclestones. His house was in the terraced row that backed onto these. Not Minty's attacker, not some vicious rapist. 'You've got it all wrong.' I pulled away. 'I'm not a thief, I'm a private investigator. Look.' I pulled a card from my pocket and he looked at it.

'You can print this sort of thing off at home if you want to,' he said suspiciously.

'Constable Tootall, Elizabeth Slinger police station. He knows me, ring them, check.'

He paused. Handed back my card. He looked disappointed. 'So what you investigating?'

I still felt unsteady so I answered him. 'I got a call from a friend, she was in trouble but we got cut off. She lives here, I came round to see if she was home. There doesn't seem to be anyone in.'

'And the other night?'

'Assessing the neighbourhood for a client. They're thinking of buying property round here, wanted to know what it was like.'

'And what did you tell them?'

'Rash of attempted break-ins at present, not for the first time, occasional mugging.' I thought of Minty. This bastard had scared me witless and now I was justifying myself to him. Terror was turning into anger.

'Neighbourhood Watch,' he introduced himself, finally satisfied with my account.

'Not a good idea to launch yourself at people like that.'

He gave a pompous smile.

'That could be classed as assault,' I said. Too late to add over-enthusiastic vigilante to the Ecclestone's list.

His face flushed and he looked mutinous.

'Besides I might have retaliated.'

'Oh, yes?'

'Yes. Kick-boxing.' OK. I was fibbing but it sounded better than self-defence. 'Could have broken your leg, smashed your knee-cap,' I said sharply. 'You carry on like that with some kid wired up on drugs, or after a fix, he's carrying a knife...' I let him imagine the consequences.

He didn't like my attitude but then I hadn't liked being attacked by a stranger and nearly having a heart attack. I reckoned we were quits.

'I have a job to do.'

He stood aside and I stepped through the gate pulling it shut after me. I felt his eyes on me as I walked away but I resisted the urge to look back or make any childish gesture. Neighbourhood Watch was all well and good but the guy really needed some training in appropriate action. I bet the starter kit didn't advocate sneaking up on lone women in the dark and grabbing them in an arm-lock.

I was shaking. I sat in the car and leant back against the seat, my head against the rest. All my senses felt stretched, everything larger than life, the pear-drops taste in my mouth, the smell of plastic in the car, the sound of my breath, the feel in my windpipe as though it had been scoured. And there was a giddy sense of relief and abandon. I was alive, I was fine, I was safe.

Chapter Sixteen

When I'd calmed down enough I tried Minty's number again. Still no answer. I fumbled putting the key in the ignition, my co-ordination off-kilter. I drove slowly not trusting my reflexes. My route home took me back down Severn Road. Perhaps I'd run over Mr Neighbourhood Watch on the way. The thought made me giggle.

I scanned the road. Minty might be around here if her assailant had jumped her like before, close to home. Or maybe she'd seen him and was hiding. Why not call me again? Because he might hear? Each time I passed a gateway or ginnel where she might be I slowed. But I didn't see anyone.

When I reached the gloomy Smiths' house I saw the front door was ajar. I closed my eyes and swore softly. It was a perishing night, the cold would be unbearable with the door open. Had someone broken in? I couldn't ignore it so I tried to focus on my choices. Just thinking clearly seemed such an effort. And of course I wasn't thinking clearly; I was tired and shaken-up and all over the place. What could I do – phone the police or check it out myself? How long would it take the police to come? It would depend on what else was kicking off in Manchester. An open door wasn't exactly a serious crime, it would probably mean waiting for them. So – sit and freeze and worry or act and likely be home drinking hot cocoa in quarter of an hour?

What if there were burglars in there? Stealing what exactly? It was hardly a prime target. More likely to be a rough sleeper, I told myself, someone desperate for shelter, or even more simply the door hadn't closed properly the last time someone had been out, the wood might have warped with the change in weather, the latch might be broken. I reassured myself with these thoughts but if I'm honest there was also a need to regain some ground – to be brave and face down the demons.

Taking my torch from the back seat, I tucked my mobile in my pocket and made my way through the weeds past the rusting car and up the two broad stone steps to the doorway I shone the light inside, it illuminated a drab hallway. Piles of circulars and free newspapers were scattered about.

I called out loudly, 'Hello, hello.' If there were prowlers I didn't want to sneak up and surprise them. And I didn't want to frighten Mr and Mrs Smith. 'Hello, the door's open, hello?'

Silence. Deep, dull silence. I must have listened for two minutes and there wasn't a breath of noise.

I looked at the door. The lock was broken but it was impossible to tell whether that was recent. I took a couple of steps inside still calling out, feeling a little foolish but keen not to surprise anyone. The place reeked of damp and rotten wood, a mouldy, mushroom smell that reminded me of grubbing in the woods as a child. I pointed the torch up the stairway. A swirl of fear. I didn't want to go up there. Mrs Smith wouldn't manage those stairs, would she? I bargained with myself – if they weren't downstairs then I would definitely let the police handle it.

I swung the beam round and picked out three doorways on the ground floor, the front room nearest to me and two others at the back; kitchen and dining room, I guessed.

I stood and listened some more. My hands were getting numb. I could see an old light switch, the round sort dating from decades before, they'd long since been replaced in most homes. Probably illegal now. There was a bulb above at the end of curly brown cables. I tried it but nothing happened.

When I knocked on the lounge door it swung open. No bulb in the ceiling fitting here. The room was deserted, a lumpen sofa and a rickety Formica table the only furniture. The walls were decorated with a faded floral pattern, bunches of wisteria. There were blooms of mildew in patches and spongy fungus sprouting in one corner of the ceiling. Yellow curtains were nailed across the big front window. The fireplace was open and the grate full of rubbish. I could hear something rattle in the chimney, then silence.

I followed the torch beam down the hall to the door at the back. I knocked and called out again. 'Mrs Smith, hello?' They might be asleep, hard of hearing.

In the kitchen the back door was broken in, wood splintered and torn back, just enough to gain entry. So someone had broken in. And then what ... found nothing and left by the front door? Who'd be desperate enough to burgle here? Junkies?

There were scraps of food rotting on the table and bags of rubbish which something, rats I thought, had torn open and scattered. The room smelt stale. A pre-war gas cooker stood beside an original deep Belfast sink. I shone my torch in the sink. It was bone dry, the bottom dusty as though it hadn't seen any water in years. I turned the tap. Nothing. How did they cope without water? The squalor was appalling but my revulsion was tempered with anger. How could they live like this and no one care, no one help? First thing in the morning I'd be onto Rachel again – if the Smiths weren't known to Social Services they should be.

I knocked on the dining room door, called out and went in. The smell made me gag, saliva flooded my mouth and my throat convulsed. They must have been using it as a toilet. I was right. My torch lit upon an old pan and a bucket, brimful. I jerked the beam away, across to the window at the back, a mattress below, old clothes piled on it in bin liners, torn with streaks of something showing. Ahead. Fingers. The hand swollen, the colour of aubergine. The cheek, skin splitting, exposing mottled lumps, jagged edges, white shapes. Oh god no. Not bin liners. A man. A corpse. Mr Smith, curled on his side, his face torn open.

I dropped the torch, gasped in the sudden dark and breathed in the foul air again. It stuck in my throat like powder, bitter and rank. I scrabbled for the torch and as I raised it the torchlight picked out the heel of Mrs Smith, the broken shoe, she lay face down in all the clothes I'd seen her in. Vomit rose in my throat. I clenched my teeth tight, pressed my tongue hard against the roof of my mouth.

'Mrs Smith?' My voice was squeaky. I took a step closer. The smell was unbearable. I pulled my fleece up over my nose, breathing in the smell of my clothes and deodorant. I didn't want to touch her but if she was still alive ... I squatted down, I put out my hand, trembling uncontrollably and touched hers. It was stone cold and without moving it I could feel the dense weight, the solidity of rigor mortis. I stumbled up and turned away and was sick, hot and sour, all over the floor.

Wiping my mouth with the back of my hand I hurried to the front door. My legs didn't work properly, like running in soft sand. My teeth were chattering and my bowels burned. I got in the car and locked the doors, terrified that I'd be next. A hand on my shoulder, breath on my cheek. My heart hammered hard. I whirled round to check there was no one hiding in the back seat.

I drew out my phone, had to stab at it twice to release the keypad lock, my fingers seemed bigger than normal. Pressed 999.

They came quickly. Uniforms and an ambulance then detectives from the serious crime squad. A stream of people asked me the same questions which I answered as best as I could. But I was cold and empty and deeply shocked by the violent scene I'd walked into and it was so hard to keep track of what they were asking and to find the right words to answer them.

Every time I closed my eyes there was a sequence running, the cone of light rippling over the darkened corpse, Mr Smith's face, Mrs Smith's dirty heel, her clumps of hair. And I could smell them on me, rotting meat and shit. To die like that. The images blurred when tears finally found me. Who were the tears for – them or me?

At last they let me go. One of them explained to me that they couldn't tell yet what had happened to the Smiths.

'It's not clear yet whether anyone else was involved.'

'Someone broke in.'

'Yes, but there are no obvious signs of violence.'

I struggled with that. Wasn't the whole place redolent with violence? I shook my head.

'No wounds, no blood loss.'

The images spooled round in my head. I ran the loop. Stopped at the frame, the moment before I'd dropped my torch. 'His face, his cheek...' Torn, glimpses of jaw, teeth.

'Animals...'

Rats.

'...they go for the soft tissue. Could have happened ... after.'

I grimaced.

'We'll talk tomorrow.'

They believed me when I said I was safe to drive. I left them sealing off the premises with stripy tape and unloading equipment from a van. I crept home, driving like a learner, checking the mirror all the time, signalling carefully even though there was scarcely any traffic about. My breath coming in misty clouds, my nose numb, my fingers rigid. Expecting to crash at any moment.

Chapter Seventeen

The first thing I did at home was brush my teeth and wash my face, trying to get rid of the taste and the smell. I had a raging thirst and drank a large glass of water.

Television sound came from the lounge,

Ray was still up, watching a movie.

'Hiya,' he said without looking back, 'you took your time. Steve Buscemi – he's brilliant in this...' he nodded to the screen.

'Ray,' a little squeak, I sounded about six years old.

He turned round, alarm shot across his face, he began to get up. 'What's up?' He took a step towards me.

'Don't.'

'What?'

'I smell. Oh, Ray.'

'Come here,' he put his hand on my elbow, led me to the sofa and sat me down.

Tears spilt down my cheeks, ran into the corners of my mouth. He put his arm around me and I let my face sink into his chest. I was grateful and embarrassed but mainly I was horribly, endlessly sad. He held me while I told him the story, a jerky account in fits and starts. Then I cried some more.

'I'm sorry,' I'd finally stopped and I pulled away. I shuddered. 'Your shirt's all wet.' I stroked the wet cotton. Felt his heart bump, the heat of him. I glanced up. He had a peculiar look on his face. I felt a rush of desire, physical, tightening, dizzying. I wanted him to touch me, undress me, kiss me, make love to me. His lips parted. I moved my hand away. I could see the pulse in his throat. The moment hung in the air like a promise. His eyes were fixed on me, dark eyes, the pupils huge. Like a well to fall into. He moved his head a fraction towards me. Gentle pressure on my back. My breasts were against his ribs, my nipples were tingling. I took a breath. My stomach plunged. Oh, Ray.

'Sal,' he whispered. His voice was thick. He wanted me. His lips grazed mine.

Oh, Ray. I mustn't. It was wrong.

'Could do with a drink.' I stood up, unsteady. It was like being in a dream, tilting into a different scene. 'Something strong. Brandy.'

Emotion flashed across his face. Anger, disappointment, relief? I couldn't tell. Please, I thought, don't say anything. Please, pretend it never happened. Nothing happened. Nothing.

He regarded me for an age. Then, 'Ice?'

I smiled and worked hard at not crying again.

We both had a tumbler of the stuff and I filled the space with more details from my evening, aware that Ray was listening but also that he was watching me closely, daring me to admit the attraction there now was between us, an edge of intensity in his gaze and I was conscious of him, every time he shifted the glass in his hands, the shape of his hands.

'I said I'd be here tomorrow, to give a statement. There will be an inquest – with it being sudden death.'

'I can do school.'

'Don't need to pick them up,' I remembered. I told him about the arrangements. 'It's really late,' I drained my glass. 'I need a soak, get warm.' Try to get rid of the smell.

'Okay.' He stayed where he was while I got up. Watching me unashamedly. I felt clumsy and so confused. Punch drunk. The moment's intimacy coming on top of the horrors I'd witnessed had knocked me sideways.

I ran the bath, adding rose and lavender oils, inhaling the sweet aromas in the steam. Soothing, it claimed on the label. Ray and I were friends, companions, housemates. He had a steady girlfriend, for heaven's sake. I didn't fancy him, I'd never fancied him, not really. He had a moustache. I didn't rate moustaches. He wasn't my type. And even if he was it would be wrong to get involved. Who'd started it? Was it my fault? Crying all over him and needing comfort? Comfort not anything else. It was when I touched his chest. That heat. I wanted to pull open his shirt, press my palms flat against him, hold my cheek against his ribcage. Drink in his heartbeat. I pulled away from the fantasy. What was his excuse? A momentary aberration? Knee-jerk reaction to having a woman in his arms? Didn't make sense. He didn't play around, he'd never cheated on anyone in all the years I'd known him. And he'd never made a move on me before. We already had a relationship and sex was no part of it.

The water was hot, raising goose bumps on my skin at first. Hot. I never wanted to be cold again. My insides were still chilled through. We didn't do anything, I told myself. Not even a kiss. Semantics. If I'd listened to my body and not my mind we would have gone on, a kiss and more ... that look in his eyes, sullen with desire. Oh, God! Why had it felt so wrong? Because it might mess everything up?

I leaned back and let the water soak my hair and fill my ears. I sat up and slathered on shampoo, fell back and rinsed it off. I used the loofah to scrub at my arms and legs. Now and then my mind rolled back to the Smiths' house. A collage of what I had witnessed and the terrible narratives I imagined to account for their deaths. I tried not to resist, to let it roam where it needed and begin the process of recovering from the shock.

Tucked up in bed I listened to the familiar sounds of the house and for the first time in all the years we'd known each other I wondered whether Ray would come to my room. And what I'd do if he did.

Chapter Eighteen

I woke early with a dry throat and a stiff neck. It was only a matter of seconds before images from the night before flooded through me: the bloated corpse, buckets of human waste, *I'm scared*, Minty's call, *bit of explaining to do, haven't you,* the smell of onions, *animals, they go for the soft tissue.* Ray! A swoop of guilt in my stomach out of all proportion. An awkward moment, that's all. I probably misread it all, I was in such a state. Nevertheless I stayed in bed avoiding him and only surfaced to kiss Maddie goodbye when she came looking for me.

'You're going to Katy's for tea.'

'Aw.'

I hadn't the capacity to deal with any more of her messing about. 'It's all arranged,' I said firmly, 'Tom's going to Adam's so Ray and I will both be working; we can't pick you up.'

I had a shiver of anxiety as she disappeared, my fears slopping over from work to taint the everyday areas of life. I squashed the impulse to run after her – she needed consistency, not to be burdened by my lurches of emotional insecurity. I came to regret my restraint. Things might have turned out so differently if I'd gone after her, given her another hug, that extra chance to say something. Changing that moment might have had a ripple effect on everything else. That day and the ones that followed might have taken another and less damaging course.

After a childish breakfast of coddled eggs and soldiers and freshly squeezed orange juice I got myself dressed. I put on the local radio station and caught the news. Nothing about the Smiths. It was a gloriously sunny day but the easterly wind persisted and I kept the central heating on. The forecast was for change by the end of the day, warmer wetter weather to replace the record-breaking cold spell we'd had.

When I heard knocking I assumed Ray had forgotten to take his key and tried to assume an innocent, practical, girl-next-door look. I needn't have bothered. Two men in suits stood on the doorstep, detectives. They wanted to talk to me about the previous evening. I let them in, ushered them past the clutter of boxes in the hall. They looked round the lounge with quite blatant curiosity. I had a flash of the old TV detective Columbo doing the same, finding out all sorts of damning information from someone's knick-knacks.

I offered drinks, which they refused.

'Have they done the post-mortems?' I asked the older man. He had a froggy look to him, wide mouth, bulging eyes. He swivelled his eyes my way. Frowned.

'The officer last night, I can't remember his name, he said it might take a couple of days.'

'What time was this?'

'I don't know exactly. He had a bit of a stammer.'

There was an awkward pause. The frog-man looked at the other one who was pointy and anaemic looking.

'No signs of violence,' I said, elaborating for them. 'But someone had broken in the back. They couldn't be really sure until they'd done the post-mortems. I don't know how fast they do them.'

Another uncomfortable silence.

'What's wrong,' I said, 'was it murder? Oh, god, was there someone upstairs?!'

The pointy man cleared his throat. 'You were in Old Landsdowne Road last night?'

'Yes.' I was puzzled. 'Just before I found them.'

'What were you doing there?'

'Why?'

'We've received a complaint. You were trespassing and when you were challenged you became abusive and made threats.'

Heat flooded my cheeks and my temper flared. Mr Neighbourhood Watch.

'That's ridiculous, the man assaulted me, he jumped on me – did he tell you that?'

'Have you reported it?' Pencil Nose said dryly.

'No. He half-strangled me.'

'But you–'

'I was rather busy dealing with two dead bodies.'

That shut them up.

But not for long.

'What were you doing at Old Landsdowne Road?' Froggy growled.

'Calling on a friend,' I said baldly. I didn't want to explain any more; things were complicated enough.

'This friend's name?'

'Minty.'

He waited.

'I don't know her surname.'

He pursed his fleshy lips.

'She's a new friend.'

He looked at his buddy then back to me. 'This friend,' he put it in inverted commas, 'can vouch for you then?'

I shut my eyes. I didn't want them traipsing round there in their size twelve's but what could I do? 'Sure,' I breezed, 'ask her.' Hoping they'd better things to do than take this any further. When Froggy let slip a sigh I got the impression he was with me on that.

'There have been a number of break-ins in the area–' Pencil Nose began.

'And you think I've got anything to do with that?' I retorted. I was furious, heat in my head and a rush of rage through my chest. And then instead of letting loose with a barrage of scathing comments I found to my complete horror that I was crying. Instead of snapping I'd burst, well, leaked anyway, and I could feel my face getting blurry and red as the two men shifted uncomfortably.

At that moment Ray came in.

'Sal?'

Shit, shit, shit. 'It's all right,' I wailed.

'I think you'd better leave,' Ray sounded deadly, like he'd suddenly uncovered his Mafia roots.

'Police,' I told him.

'Look at the state of her,' he accused them.

The frog man made to speak but I interrupted. 'I'm fine.' My shoulders soughed up and down like old bellows and I tried to stop crying. I wiped at my nose and face. The old couple in that ghastly room, this was so petty, the thought set me off again.

Ray put his arm around my shoulders. I could feel the heat of it, the weight. I wanted to move away but the police might think it strange.

'She plays Good Samaritan and this is what she gets,' Ray's lips were white with rage, his nostrils wide.

'Wrong police,' I tried to explain.

More knocking at the door. Ray swore in

Italian and went to answer it.

'I think we can leave it there,' the pointy man said crisply. 'We'll call back if there's anything else.'

'If I had been up to no good,' I put in my two penn'orth, 'and that stupid man had gone for me like he did then you'd probably be dealing with GBH now. Any self-respecting scally would have hospitalised him. He needs warning. He's a liability.'

The door opened and another two suits appeared. They all seemed to know each other and made little grunts and gestures like a pack of dogs exchanging greetings. The first two left and the next two settled down. I had stopped bawling. Ray remained scowling by the door.

'It's okay,' I told him. I didn't want a chaperone. He didn't budge.

I turned back to the men. 'This is about Mr and Mrs Smith,' I checked. They nodded.

My phone trilled and I glanced at the display. Lucy Barker. I bowed my head. Oh no. Not now. Had Benjamin caught up with her? 'I need to take this, I'm sorry.'

She was fine, just eager to know if I'd found Benjamin yet. I told her I was still waiting to hear and would be in touch.

Back to the policemen. 'Have they done the post-mortem?'

'Not till this afternoon but the police surgeon is pretty sure of the cause.'

'Murder?' I waited, my throat thick.

'Natural causes.'

'Natural,' I cried. 'What's natural about it?'

He pulled a face in sympathy.

I ran the loop again in my head.

I didn't want to accept it. If it was murder, there was someone to blame, a brutal, mindless killer. Someone to catch, to punish. Without that ... nothing. Who was responsible, who would bear the guilt?

'Natural?' I said again.

'Hypothermia.'

Oh, Lord. I grimaced. My eyes pricked a little. In fashionable West Didsbury, in one of the richest countries on earth. They'd frozen to death.

Chapter Nineteen

It was splashed all over the *Manchester Evening News*. Ray had reluctantly left, peeling himself away from the wall and asking me three times if I was sure before leaving me to complete my statement. The suits had gone by the time Sheila arrived home from lectures with a copy of the paper.

She didn't know I'd found the bodies. She hadn't seen me since I'd got back the night before. I managed to get through the account without bursting into tears. She made some tea and we poured over the paper together.

'The police don't know if they've any family,' she pointed out.

'Be worse if they have.' The load of shame and guilt that would land someone with.

When another caller knocked Sheila went to answer the door. It was Diane.

'Ray rang,' she said without preamble, her eyes appraised me swiftly. 'I hear you've been having a hard time of it.'

'Sal found them,' Sheila held out the paper. She left us to talk and I went through it all again. I knew the telling and re-telling was part of coming to terms with the trauma and disruption. Made sense to talk but I was becoming exhausted. 'I'm all over the place,' I concluded. 'The shock.'

'You're not kidding.'

I hadn't said anything about Ray. I told Diane everything, no secrets. It kept me sane. But I was nervous. What would she say? Would she laugh? Would her reaction help me deal with my muddled feelings?

'Ray rang you,' I broached the topic.

'He sounded worried.'

'When I got in,' my stomach began to knot, 'he was still up and, well, I was devastated, and...' I stuttered to a halt. Diane regarded me closely. Loud knocking made me jump. I cursed. Let my head sink into my hands.

'Shall I go?'

'Send them away, whoever it is. I've already had to deal with two lots of police today.' A thought flashed into my mind as she was going. 'If it's someone from the papers I've gone away for a few days.'

Word of mouth is good publicity for my job but having my face splashed about the papers is not. I flexed my shoulders aware that the stress was seeking out my weak points. My neck was rigid, my left shoulder humming with slow, nagging, burning pain. I heard raised voices. Diane and another woman. Before I could respond the door flew open and a woman burst in. Blonde hair, curly, slight physique. Minty. Though her face was almost unrecognisable, a mess of cuts, swellings, red and purple marks.

'Oh my God!'

'I'm sorry,' Diane had obviously tried to stop her barging in.

I held my hands up, a gesture of surrender more than anything.

'Sit down,' I said to Minty. She took a perch on a chair, she looked broken, humiliated.

Diane was confused but realised it was my call. 'Tea?'

I nodded.

When Minty and I were alone I studied her injuries. One eye swollen shut and a vicious gouge across her eyebrow, her nose looked misshapen, the flesh puffy and shiny, her lips blue, a cut in one corner and a streak of dried blood running from one ear.

Inside things were clawing at my guts but when I spoke I sounded quite calm. 'What happened?'

She kept looking at her hands using one nail to pick at the remnants of pink varnish on her nails. Why was she here? She had called me last night – was that before this had been done to her?

'Have you seen a doctor?'

She gave her head a tiny shake.

'Was it the same man?'

Mute.

There were clumsy pauses between my questions. I wasn't functioning well myself. What did she want from me?

'I came last night after you rang. To the house. There was no answer.'

She gave a little shudder. She wore a wool jumper, three-quarter length sleeves. The hairs on her arms were erect, her skin raised in goose bumps. She was cold. I saw Mrs Smith, cold to the bone, the chill creeping up her legs, along her arms, seeping into her back and her belly and her mouth. Hypothermia. He must have died first, the animals had got to him. My stomach plummeted as I wondered if he had already been dead when I'd stopped Mrs Smith as she trudged to the shops.

'Is there someone I can call? Caroline perhaps?'

She flinched. Wrapped her arms about her waist.

'Is she at work?'

'Don't.'

'But...'

'I need a refuge,' Minty said.

I thought I'd misheard, I stared at her, slow on the uptake. I got there eventually.

'Oh, sweet Jesus!' I couldn't hide my revulsion.

'Caroline did it.'

Are you sure, I wanted to ask. Stupid. As if she could be mistaken.

Diane came back with a tray, mugs of tea, some of Sheila's homemade parkin.

Why hadn't she told me the first time? First Lucy now Minty. Everyone playing me false.

'Can I stay here?'

No way. My gut response. I'd enough on my plate without taking in an abused woman. But I felt a flush of shame, too. *You can't say no.* Ray's words when I'd set out after Minty's call.

'Women's Aid,' I mumbled.

'I cannot go to there,' she gave a little laugh, tears in her voice, 'we know some of the staff.'

Christ. I thought of all the friends at Chris's party, all the networks, the circles in the city and beyond, overlapping.

'Are you a client?' Diane was trying to make sense of the situation, she handed round the drinks.

'We met by chance,' I told Diane. 'She'd been hurt, I thought she'd been mugged. Minty rang me last night but I didn't get there in time.'

'I can't go back,' Minty said.

'Your bloke's done that to you?'

'Partner,' I said, 'Minty lives with Caroline, they know Chris and Jo. They were there on Saturday.'

'Bloody hellfire!' Diane stood with her mouth open, hands on hips. She checked my eyes for confirmation. I gave it. 'I didn't recognise you,' she said to Minty.

'Please, let me stay,' Minty said, 'I'm scared.'

I thought of Maddie, the decorating, Ray and Tom, Sheila. Work. It was a bad idea. I didn't want to let her into my home. Acknowledging it made me feel unkind.

'No,' I managed. 'We'll sort something else out.' I took a sip of tea, my hand shook lightly. 'You must see a doctor.'

She began to shake her head. I butted in. 'Don't be daft. You need to start thinking about yourself. Your nose could be broken, your eye looks terrible and those cuts – they'll heal better if they're properly treated.' And there would be a file then too. With her injuries on record. We both knew that.

'Where will I go, though?'

Had Minty any money, could she afford a B&B? I glanced at Diane. Feeling trapped.

Diane spoke. 'You can stay at mine for a bit till you can sort something out.'

Minty nodded, her mouth clenching like a child on the verge of tears. 'Thank you.'

'But there's a condition,' Diane said, 'we go to Casualty first.'

Minty's shoulders slumped. 'Not MRI, and not Wythenshawe.' She was frightened that Caroline would come after her.

'Stockport,' I said. 'Where did you go last night?'

'Just walked.'

'She let you go?'

'I hid, she set off in the car, looking...' her voice went high and thin.

'You walked all night?'

'My things are at home, I've no money or anything.' Her hand jerked and tea spilt on

225

her jeans. 'Sorry,' she said, wiping at it. 'I didn't know where to go. Caroline was tired, there's a lot of people off work with stress, she's so much on...'

'Minty. Caroline assaulted you. Don't make excuses for her.'

'Don't tell anyone, please?' She bowed her head, begging me.

I sipped my tea. 'Are you going to leave her?'

She hesitated.

'Are you going to report it?'

'I don't know.'

'How long have you been together?'

'Three years. We bought the house together.'

'Three years?'

'She didn't used to...'

Beat me?

'...just she gets so uptight, not sleeping and...'

It was a story I'd heard many times but it had always been a he before.

'We'd better go,' Diane put down her mug.

'Ring me later,' I told Diane.

Minty got to her feet.

'You could do with a coat,' I told her.

'Mine'd swamp you,' Diane observed.

I was nearer to Minty's size. I found a

fleece that I wore for walking.

'Thanks.' She put it on carefully. Sore in places that didn't show.

After they had gone I felt dizzy with fatigue. I considered lying down but sleeping in the day often led to a restless night so I compromised. I laid on the floor and did some slow breathing and stretching exercises, relaxing the stiff muscles in my back and neck and loosening the spiral of adrenalin that had plaited my guts.

I'd actually drifted off when the phone startled me. It was Rachel, the social worker.

'Sal,' she spoke softly, 'I don't know if you've heard, the couple you were asking about...'

'I found them. I was the passer-by in the reports.'

'Oh, my God. I'm so sorry. What happened?'

I explained. 'They reckon it's hypothermia.'

I heard her intake of breath.

'The place was filthy. There was no heat, no gas or electricity, the water was off too. They were using a bucket for a toilet. How can that happen?'

'If we'd only ... Sal, I don't know. Some

people don't want intervention.'

'They died like animals, Rachel, worse, there was no dignity.'

There was silence. Unusual for Rachel who's the talkative type.

'Scavengers had been at his body,' I persisted. What did I want from Rachel? She was a social worker but hardly culpable for something outside her own caseload, for the failings of the service that employed her.

'They were just left to rot.'

'You don't know, Sal. They may have chosen not to accept any help. Some people do.'

'What I saw – that wasn't a choice. It stinks,' I said.

'We don't know the history. People have to be referred or at least brought to our attention. And it happens, sadly it's not all that unusual, you know, deaths from hypothermia. People on a pension – sometimes it's a toss-up between food and heat.'

'Is that supposed to make me feel better?'

'No. But the Smiths aren't alone. And you're right: it stinks.'

'I'm sorry,' I sighed, 'I'm all over the place today. I feel so cross, and it's so sad and then I start to feel guilty.'

'Don't.'

My eyes strayed to the garden. I watched a magpie stab at the grass. 'Some people say we get the world we deserve. I don't know about that but this – it shouldn't be like this. It's not right.'

I couldn't rest after. I got a pen and paper from the computer desk, trying to distract myself, shift my worry onto Lucy Barker. Even if we sorted out the ultimatum to Benjamin I didn't trust her to come clean if he broke it. She was besotted. But what I could do was compile a summary of his actions to date which I could give to the police if it were needed.

My progress was slow, my mind drifting about but eventually I had it all in order and typed up. Dates, times and details. Three o'clock. A sudden rush of panic made me reel – Maddie and Tom – but I remembered immediately that they were out to tea. Ray would pick them up later. I didn't want to think about Ray.

It was too cold and horrible to do any gardening, my usual answer to restlessness. I looked glumly at the playroom. Half an hour? It always takes longer than I think – and more paint. I'd just started a second coat on the ceiling when the phone rang.

Katy's mum.

'Sal, we thought Maddie was coming for tea.'

'She is.' My stomach dropped like stone.

'I'm at school. We can't find her.'

Chapter Twenty

A stream of nightmares danced their way through my mind as I raced to school. Images from countless tragedies, TV newsreels, posters in shop windows, parents with tearstained faces making pleas, small coffins. I'd rung Ray's mobile and left a message: *you haven't picked the kids up have you?*

Just a mix-up, just a mix-up. Terror sang through my veins. My breath was thick, stuck like glue behind my breastbone, as if by holding onto it I could keep her safe. Just a mix-up.

The playground was deserted, I found Fiona and Katy in the reception area along with Miss Dent and Mrs Tewkes and a uniformed policewoman. There was an air of tight panic about them. My legs buckled.

I stumbled and fell against the wall. It was the uniform. People rushed to help me. I shook my head trying to clear it.

'I'm fine,' I lied.

'She's probably gone with Tom,' someone said.

'She's a sensible child,' Miss Dent reassured me.

They asked me what she was wearing. God no. I rode the adrenalin, I had to stay strong. I couldn't help Maddie if I crumbled but I could feel my heart tripping and bucking, the rhythm all wrong. I couldn't remember what she had been wearing, what if I was mistaken, told them the wrong colours? I fought to recall the morning. I had an image but I'd no idea whether it was accurate. Her red top, I think, navy trousers, powder blue, fur-trimmed Eskimo coat, black ankle boots – nubuck.

Ray rang.

'Maddie's missing. Ring Adam's, see if Tom's there, if they saw her.'

I had to repeat it for him.

He grasped the seriousness of the situation, gave a terse 'right', and rang off.

'She was in school till the end of the day?' the police officer asked Miss Dent.

'Yes. I didn't see her leave. The juniors can

go out into the playground as soon as they're ready,' she explained.

Why? I wanted to tear her head from her shoulders, why aren't they kept, like the little ones, until someone picks them up? Why didn't you look after her? Totally irrational, I know.

'D'you think she might have gone home?' Fiona asked.

'I'll go back there, check.'

There was a ghastly silence then several people spoke at once. Mrs Tewkes arranged to ring round all Maddie's friends. The policewoman asked for my mobile number and I left that with them. The caretaker appeared, a scouser who knew most of the kids by name. A kind man, unlike the caretakers I remembered from my school-days who'd been a cross between Attila the Hun and Frankenstein's monster.

'I'll keep lookin'. But she's not 'ere.'

I drove home offering endless prayers to unnamed gods. Why hadn't I listened to her? She hadn't wanted to go to school. If only I'd kept her home. I should have paid more attention. As well as blaming myself my mind taunted me with crazy, scary possibilities, some completely bizarre: Benjamin Vernay had got her, Caroline had kidnapped her to force Minty home.

I ran through the house calling for her. Sheila came down the top stairs from her attic flat to see what was wrong.

I explained.

'She'll be all right,' she said, her face creased with worry but her eyes calm. 'She will.' She tried to make it sound like a certainty but it could only be a hope.

Ray got back as soon as I was pulling my bike out of the shed. She'd be on foot, easier to see her from the bike than the car. Where would she go? The park? The shops? Christ, she was only seven, she never went anywhere on her own.

'The police are looking,' I kept my jaw rigid to hold everything together.

'I'll try the park,' Ray said, 'maybe Digger...'

I made a noise, a burst of laughter choked with tears. Digger was useless as far as dog skills went. He looked the part but in terms of guarding humans, chasing cats or even retrieving sticks he was a waste of space. Ray touched my elbow, trying for a gesture of comfort. I held up my hands: no. The intimacy would break me.

I cycled up and down the roads between our house and the school. It's only half-amile. I wove up and down every side road, the cul-de-sacs, the alleys. My hands numb on the handlebars and my eyes watering with the cold. Past the Fire Station, round by the old cinema, Cine City, now up for sale and up as far as Withington Library. I explored all around the shops on Copson Street and the car parks at the back, down past the swimming baths, along Oak Road and Christie's Hospital. I went into Mohammed's on the corner; he knew us well but he hadn't seen her. I asked the paper girl. I stopped people in the street trying to keep the hysteria from my voice. And I prayed, talking to her all the while, telling her how much I loved her, how wonderful she was, how she filled my life with passion and challenges, humour and pleasure. Grounded me. Made me complete.

It began to rain at five, the cold weather breaking as warmer, westerly winds pushed cloud in from over the Irish Sea. I called back at the house, Digger nearly knocked me over, keen to get out, probably thought Ray had gone walkies without him.

'Have some tea,' Sheila slid a mug across the table. 'Ray's gone back into the village.'

I cradled the mug, stood staring out at the back garden. Digger walked across the lawn wagging his tail.

'I just don't...' I broke off. Digger was by the old tree in the corner. Beside him a smudge of powder blue in the sullen light. Movement, a hood edged with fur.

I gave a little squeak, spilled hot tea over my hand as I put it down and dashed to the door. Shelia frowned at me then looked out and saw what I had.

'Oh, thank God.'

She was sitting on one of the big stones around the low bed beneath the tree. Her arms were wrapped round her knees, head bent. Digger walked back to greet me presumably feeling full of himself.

I squatted next to her and drew her close. I couldn't speak for a few moments, didn't want to break down in front of her. Had to be strong for her. Finally I tried my voice. 'Oh, Maddie. I've been so worried about you. You okay?' She gave a little nod. I sat beside her on the wet stone and pulled her up onto my knee. I could see she'd been crying. I savoured the feel of her, the weight of her on me, the warmth of her.

'People have been looking for you, we'd better tell them you're home.'

'I'm sorry, Mummy.'

'It's all right. Let's go in and get dry and

you can tell me all about it.'

Sheila made toast, more tea for me and hot chocolate for Maddie while I rang the school, the police and Ray.

Later we lay side by side on my bed, the curtains drawn, the lamps lit.

'You have to tell me what's going on, Maddie.'

'Nothing.'

'No!' I made an effort to soften my tone. 'No, you left school on your own – you know that's not safe, you know you're not allowed to do that. Tell me why.'

'I can't,' her voice tight with anguish.

'Yes, you can.'

She made snuffling noises. I rolled over and hugged her.

'You can. What was it? Something at school? Something with Carmel?'

She flinched.

'Maddie, you have to tell me.'

'No.'

'You have to,' I insisted.

'She said she'd kill me,' she blurted out.

'Who? Carmel?'

'Katy.'

'Katy! Why?'

'She hates me and she said she'd kill me and she'll kill you and it'll be my fault. She gets me into trouble and if I don't so what she says ... and she keeps picking on Carmel and she made me do it, too. I didn't want to Mummy. Really, really I didn't want to. She said she'd cut my tongue off.' The words came thick and fast, a torrent: urgent and terrified.

'When did Katy say that?'

'Lots of times. Ages and ages.'

Katy had joined the class in September. Maddie and she had made friends almost straight away.

'And if I tell her to stop she just says she'll kill me and no one will believe me. And now she'll do it...' Her voice rose and broke.

'Maddie, Maddie, you're safe. She won't hurt you. She can't. She said some very bad things but she's just trying to frighten you. I'll make sure you're safe. Nothing will happen.'

While I spoke the thump of guilt was reverberating through me. Why? Why hadn't Maddie told me, looked for my help, my protection. Why hadn't she trusted me rather that go through all this?

'Why didn't you tell me before?'

'I don't know.'

'And Miss Dent doesn't know anything about it?'

'No.'

'There I had been inviting Katy to the pictures, to tea, pushing the girls together. No inkling that Maddie was living in dread of her.

'Carmel didn't say anything about Katy?'

''Cos Katy said she'd kill her but Carmel knew I wouldn't.'

Oh, Maddie.

'But you were unkind to Carmel too, weren't you?' I checked gently. Had that all been untrue?

'Yes. I made her cry.' The memory brought fresh tears. She burrowed her face into my neck and I made shushing sounds until she quietened.

'We'll sort it out,' I said.

'Don't tell, please, Mummy.' She was panicking.

'It's the only way. That's how we stop bullies. Katy will have to stop being mean, she'll have a points card like you.'

'No, no.' She continued to protest.

'Yes. That's what we're going to do. I'm not arguing with you about it. It's the only way.'

She cried for a bit and I held her close.

'We can ask them to put Katy in the other class.'

'Could we?' The hope in her voice cut me to the quick.

'I'll talk to Miss Dent tomorrow.'

'Do I have to go to school?'

God forbid, she needed some recovery time. 'Day off – while we sort things out.'

There was tapping at my door.

'Hello?'

Ray opened it. Tom with him.

'Thought we'd have a ride to the park and back. Stopped raining. What d'you think?'

God, no. Just let me rest.

Maddie tilted her head at me. 'Will you come?'

The four of us cycled, Digger running alongside. I was tired beyond belief. The last twenty-four hours had been unremitting trauma. My limbs ached from the tension, my mouth tasted foul, my eyes felt hard and I squinted against the fading light. Maddie was ahead, legs pumping, ringing her bell. I soaked up the sight of her. She was safe: anything else I could bear.

Ray was in the kitchen when I'd finished putting the kids to bed.

'She all right?'

'Yes. It's Katy. Katy's been bullying her and egging her on to bully Carmel. A little hierarchy of bullies.'

He shook his head, exhaled.

'I never imagined...'

'Poor kid.'

'Least it's out in the open now. She's staying home tomorrow, I'll talk to the school.'

'And how are you?' His voice softer.

I shrugged. Felt prickles on my neck. 'Shattered.' I moved towards the door.

'Sal,' he followed.

'Not now.'

'Last night ...'

'Not now, Ray.' I looked away.

Maybe he was going to apologise, or explain how he thought he'd misread the situation or declare undying love for me. Whatever, I was in no shape for anything else that day.

He took a step closer. I could smell him, hear the rhythm of his breath. 'We can't just...'

'Ray, please.'

'Okay.' He let his arms fall. I could feel his eyes on me as I walked away. I didn't need to look back to see the look on his face: I could sense it. Intent, intense, hungry.

I was in bed by nine, expecting to lie awake all night, but sleep pulled me swiftly under and held me fast till nine the following morning. I didn't remember any of my dreams, best all round I'm sure.

Chapter Twenty-One

As soon as I was up I rang the school and made a lunchtime appointment to see the staff. I knew Sheila would be home and I could leave Maddie with her for an hour.

After breakfast I spent a painful fifteen minutes eliciting some hard facts about the bullying. When had it started? Almost as soon as Katy had joined school. Had the pair of them bullied anyone else apart from Carmel? No. Had Katy ever hurt Maddie physically? Yes, she bent her fingers back when Maddie tried to object. Had she done anything else? At that point Maddie had slipped from the room and come back with a grubby piece of paper folded into a rectangle. I opened it.

Carmel is a fat slug. Childish scrawl. Maddie was supposed to put it in Carmel's tray, like she had done with the other letters. Katy had written notes to Maddie too.

She'd torn them up. *Do it or I will kill you.*

Did she ever tell anyone? No. (Why? Why? Why?) But I knew why. She was scared and she was mixed up in it. I told her again what I would say at school and as soon as I had finished she escaped to the comfort of daytime television. And I escaped outside. The milder weather gave me a chance to sort out some of the damage done by the cold spell. The frost had scorched the new growth on the maple and the clematis by the back door. I removed the worst of the crispy, bleached leaves. Hopefully the plants had time to try again: there were still some tight buds giving promise.

Harry rang to tell me that he had been successful in tracing Benjamin Vernay. Vernay was working at The Tameside Royal Infirmary. Convenient for the games he was playing as it was only a few miles away from Lucy Barker's. Harry gave me the hospital address and phone number. He was in a hurry so we didn't get to exchange news. Harry is one of the people, along with his wife Bev, who I count among my close friends. We've shared family holidays together and seen each other's children grow though we don't meet as often as we used to. Time was I had a crush on Harry.

Never acted upon, of course, him being married. Was that what Ray had? A silly crush? I set the number for Dr Vernay on one side. I didn't intend to work on the case until the following morning.

When I arrived at school for my lunchtime appointment, Maddie's teachers were as shocked as I had been at the revelations. There was a faint air of embarrassment in the meeting as we all had to re-assess our view of the situation. To her credit Mrs Tewkes took the initiative to act swiftly. Katy would change class at the end of the week and she would find herself put on the same regime that Maddie had been allocated.

That afternoon I persuaded Maddie to help me do more painting. After an hour and a half we had a turquoise box. We left it to dry, cleaned ourselves up and headed into town to get fabric for the curtains. Abakhan's on Oldham Street is a Manchester institution. Downstairs they sell fabric by weight: offcuts, seconds, end rolls. Everything from taffeta to ticking. We found some pale gold twill with a soft sheen to it that would lighten the effect of the turquoise. It had a bold, showy feel to it, reminding me of circuses or theatres.

Round the corner at Fred Aldous' craft shop we bought some gold spray to paint some of their furniture and boxes.

By bedtime Maddie was worn out, as planned. I didn't want her lying awake worrying about school. She went off to bed fine and fell asleep listening to her tape.

When I went downstairs Laura was there. I felt myself blush.

'Sal, how are you? Ray told me.'

God, no! Panic riddled through me until sense kicked in and I realised she meant about Maddie or even about discovering the bodies.

'Been better,' I managed. Ray was looking my way. I ignored him. It didn't take me long to see he was sulking. He's always been good at it but I hadn't seen him give Laura the full treatment before. It was ghastly. He refused to go out for a drink then complained through the programme on television. I excused myself and retreated to my room but couldn't settle. When I tried to escape into a book my mind skittered about like marbles on parquet flooring. I went down to fetch the material for the curtains and my sewing box. Ray and Laura were arguing in his room. Their voices were muffled and Laura was doing most of the talking. I felt sick. Not long ago I'd panicked about how close they were getting, fretting that Ray and Tom might move out and become a nuclear family, leaving Maddie and me in the lurch. Now I was disturbed to think that they might split up and that I might be to blame. I didn't want that to happen. Did I? I imagined Ray and me as an item, greater intimacy, kissing, touching, making love. I was alarmed at how my body warmed with excitement at the thought. An eddy of guilt made the whole idea murky and confusing. I grabbed the stuff I needed and went quickly upstairs and rang Diane. Minty was still there and no trouble.

'How are you?' Diane asked me.

'Shitty,' I said honestly. 'Are you busy tomorrow? Go for a drink?'

'Yer on,' she replied.

I measured and cut the fabric for the curtains and the lining and pinned them together ready for sewing. I put the radio on while I worked: Radio 3, an eclectic music programme which featured sounds from around the world. When I'd done my pinning I folded the curtains and got ready for bed.

Tomorrow I'd sort out Benjamin Vernay and finish my work for Lucy Barker. I felt as though life had been running rings around me lately. I needed to feel back in control. Work was the easiest place to start.

How wrong can you be?

Maddie faced school with surprising equanimity. We didn't see Katy, perhaps she too was having a day off in the face of the revelations. Tom and I took Maddie up and then I went with Tom to his class, exchanged his reading book, and tried to persuade him to stop hopping about and sit on the carpet to wait for his teacher. He didn't pay me any attention until I hissed, 'She's coming!' Then he sat down. In his previous school report he'd been asked to come up with an assessment of something he'd got better at. *'Sitting on the carpet'*, he'd written. I know discipline is an issue especially with thirty children to a class, but honestly! It struck me that kids like Tom needed more space to play and run about and learn through challenging physical activity. A couple of sessions of carefully supervised PE per week and playtime in a dreary tarmac wasteland wasn't really enough.

At my office I'd no sooner finished opening the mail (Insurance reminder, Credit Card offer, AA promotion) than

Lucy Barker was on the line.

'Apparently he's in Tameside, at the Royal Infirmary,' I told her, 'I'll confirm that before I send the letter.'

She gave a sharp intake of breath.

'It'll be all right,' I said. 'He'll have the letter by tomorrow morning and he'll know the game's up.'

'Thank you,' she said before she rang off. I think it was the first time that she'd ever thanked me and it surprised me.

'Tameside Royal Infirmary,' the switchboard answered the phone.

'Doctor Vernay...' I began.

'Which department?'

'I'm not sure, I–'

There was a clunk as though she had dropped the phone, I heard someone laughing and a voice explaining that someone needed a GP referral. Then a voice in my ear again. 'Putting you through.'

'E.N.T.,' a woman answered.

'Does Doctor Vernay work there?'

'Sorry?'

'Is this the right department for Doctor Vernay?'

'Is this a patient?'

'No. I need to write to Doctor Vernay, I

just wanted to check he was still with you.'

'You a G.P.?'

I was tiring of the third degree. 'Have I got the right department?'

'Can I take your name?'

'Sal Kilkenny.'

'I'll put you on hold.'

The line went dead. No muzak or blast of classical opera. I waited in the silence until I heard the warbling noises that meant I'd been disconnected. Should I try again? Before I'd geared up for it my phone rang.

'Sal Kilkenny Investigations.'

'Who are you?' A man's voice, tight with irritation.

'Sal Kilkenny. And you are?'

'Doctor Benjamin Vernay.'

Uh-oh.

'What's going on? What do you want with me?' He sounded belligerent.

'I'm working for a client, Dr Vernay. I believe you have been harassing her and I will be sending you a letter of intent. If you ignore the letter we will be seeking a legal injunction.'

'You bloody fool,' he said.

'Don't threaten me,' I said and put the phone down. I didn't seriously think he'd turn his attentions to me but direct aggression is always disturbing and it forced me from my chair to pace about the small room waiting for my heartbeat to slow and the flush of adrenalin to subside.

When the phone rang again I waited a few rings before answering.

'Sal Kilkenny.'

'I need to talk to you,' Doctor Vernay said.

I remembered the knife in the bed, the box of faeces, Lucy's bleeding fingers. 'I don't think that's appropriate.'

'It's Lucy Barker, your client, isn't it? I don't know what she's been saying but she's a liar. She's dangerous, too. I need to know where she is and what she's been doing.'

I knew she lied but dangerous? 'She's my client, confidentiality...'

'Can be waived when a person is at risk of harming themselves or others.'

'Dr Vernay, we simply want you to stop the hate campaign.'

'What!' he was incredulous. I held the receiver further from my ear. 'You've no idea what you're dealing with. What's she said about me? That I used to beat her? That I abducted her? Plied her with drugs?'

'No.' I frowned and immediately regretted getting drawn into the conversation.

'Look, I can't do this over the phone.

You're in Manchester, aren't you? I'm off in twenty minutes. I could come to you.'

'No.'

'Come to the hospital, then. The canteen.'

'All I need to do is post this letter.'

'No!' He insisted. 'You've no idea what you've got yourself into. I haven't been harassing Barker, she's been harassing me. Stalking me for the past five years. And now she's got you to do the dirty work for her.' Emotion cracked his voice. 'You damn well need to know my side of things. The damage you might have done—'

He sounded completely convincing and warning bells sounded at some of the claims he made about Lucy. Could I have got it so wrong?

'Please,' he said. 'Just think about it – have you any shred of proof about these allegations? Isn't it all based on what she's told you?'

The letters, the knife. Evidence but not proof.

'If you don't come here, I'm coming there. You have to listen to me.'

The last thing I wanted was him turning up on my doorstep, distressed and possibly deranged. I rationalised that a hospital canteen was probably about the safest place to meet him. A public place, his place of work. I'd be on alert for any threatening move and if I felt anxious I could simply give him the letter and leave it at that. I was nauseous with dread and doubt.

Chapter Twenty-Two

Tameside Royal Infirmary is in Stalybridge. The land becomes hillier as the roads climb out of Manchester, through Ashton-under-Lyne, into the western foothills of the Pennines. I journeyed through old mill towns left high and dry by the collapse of manufacturing. The lucky ones had been re-invented as dormitory towns for affluent Manchester professionals. People who work in the city but want fresh air and a glimpse of farm animals for their kids rather than the edgy hustle of city life.

Other areas lacked the views or the train station and never made the transition. Here the stolid ranks of workers housing clung to the hillsides, tiny two up two downs with tiny backyards, left to fester and decay. Once the streets here were the heart of the community. The place where neighbours gathered and shoals of children (every kid old enough to walk was part of the gang) surged this way and that. Now the streets were just the way out of town.

Tameside Royal Infirmary was a Victorian heap surrounded by a rash of prefabs and ill-matched add-ons. The main building was immense and furnished with elaborate brickwork and fancy folderols. Its imposing stature had been designed to proclaim its power over life and death.

The canteen was a dismal space: the walls were painted in heavy, creamy gloss paint and the air was thick with the scent of hot fat and onions. The staff all looked sick and overweight. I queued for coffee and asked the cashier if she knew whether Doctor Vernay was in. She pointed her chin at a man in the far corner. I wouldn't have recognised him from the photo. He now had a dark beard and a receding hairline. He wore narrow-rimmed, rectangular glasses. He was slighter than I'd imagined, scrawny looking. I took my change and went over to him. His hands were resting on the edge of the table, no knives or axes. I introduced myself and sat opposite him. He licked his lips and I realised that he too was nervous.

'You're a private detective?'

'Yes.'

'And she hired you to find me?'

'Not initially.' I hesitated, how much to divulge? Another problem.

'Let me guess,' he said bitterly, 'someone following her? Nuisance calls? Threatening letters?'

I stared at him. You should know, I thought.

'Poor little Lucy.'

I began to protest but he spoke across me. 'Always the victim. Did she tell you about her hard life? What was it this time? Brought up in care or her broken home? Mother's on the game, father's an alcoholic, locked her in her room.'

I shook my head frowning. I didn't like his tone. This time? What did that mean?

'What did she tell you about her parents?'

I couldn't see any harm in disclosing that bit of information.

'They'd emigrated.'

He laughed; a harsh, dry sound. 'They're in Barnsley. Quiet, decent, hard-working. How they ever... You'll find them in the phone book, you can ring and check. People do now and again. They've got used to it. People who finally cotton on to the truth but need some sort of reassurance. They ring the Barkers and get put in the picture. She's very plausible, Lucy, give her that. Always alone, struggling bravely on, dogged by horrendous bad luck. You'll have heard some of that, won't you: illnesses, tragedies, accidents.'

The bombing that had killed her grandfather, her brother's addiction. The rape. Didn't I believe her? Had that been a story, too? I was uncomfortable with the notion. It seemed the very worst sort of pretence in a world where women weren't believed, didn't dare to report it and when they did summon the courage to prosecute they often left even more traumatised.

'She mentioned a car crash, with you.'

His eyes swiftly filled with tears. He turned away. 'Did she now?' he said softly. 'What did she say?'

'You were engaged, you'd been to the theatre and you'd become jealous, you took a bend too fast and went into a wall. She was trapped and they had to cut her out.' As I spoke his face was flickering with small muscular contractions; he was flinching as if the memory was still too raw. 'You had some sort of concussion and wandered off. After that you went into hospital.'

He nodded, he cleared his throat. Across the canteen I heard a burst of laughter and a group of older people applauded one of their number. 'It was dark,' he said, 'November. I'd been out to the theatre with friends. It had been a pleasant evening. I'd recently moved. It was just after the first injunction had been granted.'

I grappled with what he'd just said. Lucy hadn't mentioned any injunctions.

'I got dropped off on the main road. It was only a hundred yards or so. You'd think ... sixth sense.' He rubbed at his temples, re-adjusted his specs. 'I never heard a thing, then the car was there. She ran me over.'

He must have seen my disbelief because he added, 'You can check that too. The police launched an investigation, they questioned her but they couldn't prove it. I hadn't actually seen her at the wheel, they never traced the car.'

In the silence that followed waves of cold fear chilled me to the core. Had I been wrong, so very wrong?

'You said the first injunction?'

'Here,' he fished in his jacket. I stiffened, still leery of an attack. He withdrew a wallet. 'I carry this now. And my staff are briefed to field calls.' He unfolded a piece of paper. I recognised the copy of the legal notice. I'd served enough of them in my time when times were hard and solicitors wanted someone to do the scud work. The details were all there. Lucy Loveday Barker. My hand shook as I returned it to him.

'I'm sorry.'

'There were several. They just served to enrage her.'

'But why did she?' I let the question dangle.

His look was one of complete resignation. He had no answer. Had given up on searching for one.

'Were you ever engaged?'

He shook his head. 'She was an outpatient. Came into A&E with some mystery illness. It started then. Bombarded me with letters, visits, presents. She'd turn up at work, at my home. I've moved twice.' He ran his hands over his head, pressing the short, coarse hair against his skull. 'She gets very aggressive. I sought legal advice. She doesn't care. She's even done a stint in prison.'

My mouth dropped open.

'Oh, yes. It doesn't matter to her. It's all attention. She has to be in the middle, creating a stir, at the centre, the more dramatic the better.'

'So the letters she's been getting, the break-ins...'

He watched me think it through.

'She did it herself? No,' I laughed. It was preposterous. The paint sprayed on the walls, the dogshit, the knife, her tears?

'Got your attention, playing the victim, got you on her side.'

And no one had ever seen her tormentor at the flats, the alarm hadn't gone off when they'd broken the kitchen window. There was no intruder. I stared at him. 'Then she finally told me she suspected you. She begged me not to go to the police.'

He nodded, gave a sour laugh.

'We agreed to write.' I turned away, gazed across the canteen, wrestling with the mess, looked back at him. 'I don't understand. If it was just a way of finding you then why not simply hire me to trace you in the first place? She could have told me you were a long-lost relative, or an old friend.'

'Not dramatic enough? The charade, the drama, tragedy queen. It's always a big production. Nothing's ever mundane or straightforward.'

My coffee was cooling. I took a sip; it was very bitter and made my mouth water.

'At the beginning,' he said, 'A&E – she

257

kept turning up with cuts and bruises, a broken wrist, obviously badly beaten. Her boyfriend, she said. I suggested she go into a hostel, get out of the relationship. The next week she turned up just as I was coming off shift. She'd packed a bag. She was coming home with me. She talked as if we'd been planning it for months. Like there was something between us. I put her straight. Paid for a taxi to take her to the refuge. She was back the following day. Stab wounds to her arms.'

'Oh, God.'

He leant back, pulled at his beard.

'There was no boyfriend? Lucy?'

He nodded. 'She could have come in with chest pains, dizzy spells, stomach ache – we'd have still seen her. But it wasn't sensational enough for her.'

'Has she ever seen anyone, had treatment?'

He shook his head. 'She's fine, it's the rest of the world that's the problem. She can't see that there's anything wrong. She has no feelings for anyone else, no, empathy, no shred of remorse. Psychopathic in the true sense.'

It was a nightmare. I exhaled. Took another acrid sip. My stomach felt as sour as the drink.

'I'm sorry, she seemed so ... some things felt odd, off-kilter but I never imagined this. I believed her.' I shook my head. 'It still seems such a stupid way of trying to find you.'

'None of it's logical,' he replied, moving to rest his arms on the table. 'She wants to trap me, own me. But even if she got all that, suppose I declared undying love, proposed, she'd change the game then, raise the stakes. She thrives on disharmony, adversity. She won't change.'

'I fell for it.'

'She's the best liar I've ever met. Breath-taking really. And she'll never stop. Not till they lock her up.' He pinched at the bridge of his nose. Clenched then relaxed his eyes. Sat back. 'Tell her you can't find me, tell her I've emigrated, been reported missing, anything! And get rid of her while you still can.'

Bile rose in my stomach and I gripped the edge of the table. I wanted to disappear, I wanted to travel back till before I ever set eyes on Lucy Barker. I wanted to kneel and grovel in front of Benjamin Vernay.

He studied me, his eyes old beyond his years, his thin face taut with anxiety.

'What?'

'I'm so sorry, I really am. I don't ... Lucy knows you're working here. I told her. I'm so sorry.'

Any remaining colour drained from his face. His eyelids flickered, they were almost transparent and laced with delicate blue veins. He jerked forward and gave a rough groan, a wordless protest. His eyes climbed back to mine begging for denial but finding only guilt.

'I'll call her,' I rummaged for my phone, 'I'll tell her the place was wrong say it was Thames, Thames Valley or something. That this was a dead end.'

His eyes were bright with misery now. He shook his head. Too late.

'I'll have to go.'

'But if I tell her?'

'She'll just lie down and roll over?' He spoke cynically. 'No.' Then the reality hit him again and his face contorted. 'God, no.' He ran his hands across his head again. Nearby, people glanced over wondering what bad news he was receiving.

'At least I can try,' I switched on my phone and when she answered I forced practicality into my voice. 'Lucy, I was wrong. I've been checking the address and it's not Tameside Royal, he's not on the staff here. I must have

260

misheard. It could be Teesside or maybe Thames Valley, I'm trying those next.'

'Okay,' she said. 'You'll let me know?'

'Yes, of course.' I ended the call.

'I need to go, I need to pack.'

'She won't know your home address, you'll be ex-directory?'

'It won't take her long. Once she knows where to look. This is all she does. This is her life's work.' A little laugh. 'Destroying mine. That's all that matters to her. She'll leave wherever she is, if she's working she'll walk out, she'll dump her house, everything. She's done it before.'

I thought of Lucy's flat, the incongruity I'd noticed between her attire and the lack of care in the decor and furniture. Because it was only a stepping stone in her quest.

He stood up to leave.

'She seemed to believe me then,' I said, to comfort myself as much as him.

He raised his eyebrows. 'I'm not taking any chances.'

'Is there anything I can do?'

'Think you've done enough, don't you?'

I didn't have the gall to reply. He walked away.

I took a mouthful of cold coffee and spat it back into the cup. A chill of fright washed through me then I felt an edge of rage building. Fury at Lucy Barker. Dragging me into this mess, crying victim when all the time she was the violent one, the poisonous one. I'd report her to the police? Surely if I told them about the existing injunction and her attempt to use me to trace Vernay they would act. It was evidence of her continuing obsession and there was a law against stalking. Had she broken any laws in her dealings with me? I'd find out, do her for that too. Yes, I'd get the police, get them to detain her.

The car park was surrounded by trees in bud. Low level shrubs had been planted too, glossy green hebe and mahonia, sprawling periwinkle and viburnum. In fact it looked like the car park had a bigger budget than the canteen. I stopped reversing out of my space to let another driver past. It was Benjamin Vernay, his face grim. I watched him turn left towards the exit. A second car pulled out then, also indicating left. A green Mondeo. A woman. My heart stuttered and my breath caught in my chest. No. God, no! Lucy Barker was at the wheel.

Chapter Twenty-Three

Heat bloomed across my back and neck and my mouth dried. She was after him. She must have seen right through my phone call, she had already been here or on her way. Lying in wait. I had to stop her, warn him.

I reversed sharply out and swung the car round. Where did he live? I didn't know. At the exit I scanned right and left for the two cars: one silver, one green. No sign. My heart was thumping in my chest and my palms were sticky on the steering wheel. The sun broke through the clouds and rays pierced the gloom. It illuminated everything – except where I needed to go.

I reached the roundabout. There were three exits. Where, where, where? I circled again ignoring a blast on a horn from an impatient driver. None the wiser I pulled off onto the Dukinfield exit and into the first side road. My mind was zigzagging, clutching at ideas only to drop them and move on. Could Harry find out? No time. The hospital wouldn't give out that information, only in an emergency.

It's against the law but it was my only hope. I dialled the number. 'Admin please.'

A clunk, a click and I was through.

'Sergeant Bridges here, Greater Manchester Police, Tameside Division, serious crimes. We need to contact one of your staff at home immediately, Doctor Benjamin Vernay. We believe he may be in a situation of danger to his person.' They talk like that, believe me, I've heard them. 'I'd like to get a car round there immediately but our computers are down and we can't access the system. Doctor Vernay – we need the home address.'

'Oh,' said the woman on the other end uncertainly. 'I'm not sure.'

'Your name, madam?'

'Geraldine Judd.'

'Mrs Judd, speed is of the essence. My badge number is 432D, D for Delta. Make a note of that for your own peace of mind. And I can speak to your superiors later today if required but now I really am very concerned – Dr Vernay – as quickly as possible, madam.'

'Vernay ... Vernay ... Here.' She reeled off an address in Mossley.

'Thank you for your help.'

I rang off and grabbed the A-Z. I had to peer to find the name in the warren of little roads and then work out how to get there. I backtracked to the roundabout, took the next exit and followed the Wakefield Road. My stomach was cramping with tension and I had a savage thirst. At the traffic lights a group of women with babies in strollers were waiting to cross. The lights were just on orange. I put my foot down and accelerated through. Any other time and I'd have criticised someone for driving so selfishly. I took a wrong turning at the top of the hill into a small industrial estate. Cursing, I made a three point turn and got back on track.

It was the next street. Vernay's house was halfway down. I could see his silver car but no sign of Lucy Barker's. Relief ran through me. It was okay. He was safe. Perhaps he had seen her and managed to give her the slip, or she'd got lost. I found a parking place further along and hurried to his door.

We could definitely report her now. Have her picked up straight away for breaching the terms of the injunction. Argue she was in danger of doing harm to herself or others and needed to be in custody. I thought of the lies she'd told about Ian Hoyle, the hotel manager. How he'd made a pass at her and she'd rejected him. The opposite story from his. Had she been lining him up as a new target for her deadly affection or simply diverting herself?

Look at me! Everything she did clamoured for attention. Her fire-engine red suit hiding a crimson rage, a destructive, bloody intent. Vernay was right; it wouldn't take her long to find him now she knew where he worked. Even though he'd briefed his staff, hospitals were labyrinthine workplaces and hard to keep secure. Patients records might be confidential but staff gossiped about each other non-stop and with Lucy's facility for manipulation she'd find him. Or she'd follow him home again. Stick closer. What would she do when she found him? Punish him, forgive him, start planning the wedding? It gave me the creeps and I was on the sidelines.

I rang the bell and waited. He might be afraid to answer the door if he'd spotted her earlier. I called through the letter-box, feeling slightly foolish. 'Doctor Vernay, it's Sal Kilkenny.'

I heard steps after a couple of moments. Slow steps, he was probably apprehensive. He opened the door a little. A peculiar expression on his face. I felt another flood of guilt.

'Thank God you're all right,' I said.

There was a blur of motion from behind the left of the door. He staggered back. A rush of air, a rustling noise, then a heavy thud that jolted my head, pain spread in red and white through my skull and my world snapped to black.

The first sensation after that was a block of pain pulsing through my head, surging into my teeth and jawbone, clambering down my neck, swelling in my temples. In a minute, I told myself, I'll open my eyes. What might I see? Only then did I remember where I'd been. And Lucy Barker. I opened my eyelids a fraction hoping not to alert her.

There was a carpet, a loopy texture, beige colour, I was lying on it on my side, facing into the room with the wall running along my back. I couldn't see anyone. It was a small dining room, in front of me were a table, two dining chairs and a computer chair. I listened, focused, tried to hear breathing, a sigh or a cough. A heartbeat. Heard only my own. Gingerly I tilted my head to look towards the door and the other way past my feet to the window. No one.

But the motion brought a wash of saliva to my mouth and made my stomach heave. I tried to sit up and couldn't. My hands were tied behind my back and my feet bound together. I wriggled my fingers and felt plastic rope, like washing line. I reeled with fear, felt an eddy of despair. Tears started in my eyes. I thought of Maddie, the little notes she'd sent: *I will kill you,* the ones she'd received. How had Lucy Barker become the woman she had? Had her regime of terror begun in primary school, in nursery?

I steeled myself then strained at the ropes again but they were very tight and the nausea that assailed me was so bad that I was sick on the floor. Had she heard? My heart beat wildly. Was she still here? Was Vernay? I edged away a little from the sharp smell of the vomit but I couldn't wipe my face clean. For several minutes I closed my eyes and concentrated on what I could hear. Sparrows cheeped outside, there was the slush and groan of traffic, a mobile phone trilling, the slam of a car door. People going about their business as though nothing was wrong. I resisted the swell of self-pity and tried to listen harder. Then I felt it, a small vibration through the floor, from inside the house. Someone was still here.

I had to get out, get away. She'd tied me up and she obviously wasn't going to let me go. My mind reared away at the prospect of what else she might do. And Benjamin Vernay: had she tied him up too?

Get out.

I caught the murmur of voices. His low and Lucy's shriller. Impossible to make out what they were saying.

I took stock again. Bending my head up I could see the door. It had no lock but the metal handle was quite high up. If I could get myself there would I be able to get upright to reach it – and what might happen if I opened it? At the other end of the room were a pair of wooden french windows, the old-fashioned style with lots of small panes of glass. The dining table opposite me was obviously the doctor's home office. There was a computer there. Hope leapt. Was there a phone? I couldn't really see the surface of the table. I tried to roll away from the wall and get closer but pain shot through me and made me retch again. The room grew darker and I passed out.

When I came round I could hear the sounds of someone in the kitchen, the clunk of pottery and the rattle of cutlery. My mouth was thick with thirst and my throat scorched from the acid I'd vomited. My upper arms were burning in agony. Lying on my side I rocked forward an inch or two, trying to cruise above the pain. Then I rested for a few minutes. I did it again. I used my hip, feet and shoulder to get purchase against the carpet. Little by little I edged towards the table. Eventually I could see the phone socket and double adapter in a socket under the table. Yes!!

A memory came to me: crawling between people's feet on a carpet patterned with rich swirls of red, green and gold. The tide of laughter above me. I couldn't recall the occasion but the memory was a happy one. I must have been three or four. I tried to reach beyond the fragment to find something more to savour but there was only mist.

The phone wires were tucked down behind the back of the table and one of the dining chairs. To get the phone I either needed to get up to the table or move the chair and try to pull the wire and the phone with it. I experimented with trying to get up but without the use of my arms my balance was terrible. After several attempts I got myself into a sitting position, my knees bent, feet still lashed together, hands still stuck behind my back. My whole body was trembling from the exertion. When I tried to get from there onto my knees by twisting and rocking I simply lurched forwards onto my front, creating a fresh bout of pain as I hit the floor and cracked my head again. She'd hear! Oh, please no. I shivered and tears of fear and frustration leaked out of my eyes. I sniffed them back and gritted my teeth. Get on with it! I screamed inside. You can't stop now. Just bloody get on with it! For Maddie. You must get help. Damn well do it! I wriggled forward until my head was touching the chair and then proceeded to nudge it away with the back of my head. It took forever and each time the chair tipped precariously and I was petrified that it might fall and alert Lucy Barker.

When I'd finally created enough space I edged myself up to the skirting board. The wires were close against the wall, I didn't know which was the internet connection and which the phone line. I tugged at them with my teeth and inched back and out from under the table, pulling the wires to the side. A moment's resistance and they came free, falling onto me. Both severed. She'd cut them. Devastated I lay there, pain hammering in my skull, panting with exertion and covered in a slick of sweat that made my back and arms cold.

Chapter Twenty-Four

I tried to moisten my mouth but there was no saliva. I imagined a drink; a tall, glass of cold water, sweet and slightly peaty, water from the mountains. Get me out of here, I pleaded. Please. Think. Think.

The ropes. Anything sharp enough, rough enough, to cut them? I scanned the room. The french windows. I could try to break them, use my feet. She'd hear me. Perhaps the curtains would muffle the sound a bit.

Like a caterpillar I humpbacked my way to that end of the room, my chin raw with friction from the carpet. I swivelled round till my feet were by the window then I rocked again and again until I turned myself onto my side then my back. The pain tore up my shoulder blades and into my back. Shivering uncontrollably and hopelessly weak, I breathed noisily though my mouth, making a ragged, keening sound. My first kick was feeble and my feet made precious little impact. Despair dragged at me but I took another ragged breath, pressed my lips together and tried again. I will not give up, I told myself, I will not, *kick,* give, *kick,* up. On the fifth kick I heard the creak of glass cracking. She must have heard it. But she didn't come, not then.

On the next try the glass broke more and on the seventh I heard the bright sound of smashing as it fell.

I drew my legs back, aimed to the side a bit and kicked again, sickened by the aching in my face and stomach. The small wooden frame bounced but held. Again and the wood splintered and more glass crashed. I struggled and got my feet under the curtain, thinking that there may be enough space now.

There was a scraping sound and the ground shook.

'No!' She hurled herself into the room and at me. I kicked out and broke another pane. She lunged at me. She had a hammer in her hand. I screamed, jerked my head back violently to avoid the blow. Watched her arm falling, her face brilliant with rage. The metal smashed into my shoulder. I rolled onto my side, gasping at the glow of pain radiating from the bullseye blow, the stabbing pains streaking down my arms.

'You stupid bitch,' she yelled.

I didn't move. I didn't say anything. She was dishevelled and her suit was stained; large, dark daubs. The hammer hung from her hand, glistening, wet. She came over to me and stooped and grabbed the ropes near my shins. With a strength that alarmed me she hauled me out of the room, dragging me against the carpet and bumping me through the doorway and into the lounge at the front of the house.

The smell hit me first, metal, like the taste of fresh fillings. And faeces too. For a stupid moment I was back at the Smiths' house, in the bitter cold, looking at the old man, his face torn, his flesh dark and split and spoilt with decay.

She hadn't tied Benjamin up. Hadn't needed to. There was blood everywhere. So much blood. He was on the sofa, head bowed on his chest, blooms of blood on his shirt, on his trousers and the cushions. His glasses in his lap. A stringy rope of gore hanging from the side of his head.

'Oh my God. Oh, Lucy. You've killed him. Oh, God.' I was babbling, gasping.

She glared at me, her face working

furiously. 'You shouldn't have interfered,' she cried. The marks on her suit were blood, blackish clots and splashes.

Benjamin stirred, made a small groan. Shock jolted through me.

'Call an ambulance!' I cried. 'You can save him.' Wouldn't that appeal to her sense of high drama?

I saw temptation flicker in her eyes.

'If he dies, you'll–'

'Shut up!' She swung her foot at my face. A kick to my jaw which made me swoon. The taste of blood in my mouth blended with the stink of it in my nostrils. When I looked again she was by the window, drawing the curtains, closing out the light. Shutting us off from the outside world. How late was it? Was Ray wondering where I'd got to yet? And Maddie, had school been all right? Please, I prayed, please let me go home.

Lucy Barker would kill me. How could she not? Unless I could convince her to get help.

'I thought you cared for him?'

'You don't know anything about me.'

Too right.

She stood on the rug in the middle of the room, pursed her lips, blinked. It was an expression of impatience or irritation. I

275

could see no sign of grief or terror.

'He needs help, soon. You're the only one who can help him.'

'Stop chattering,' she shook her head fiercely as though my words were insects buzzing in her ears.

I waited not wanting to provoke more violence. She still held the hammer.

Finally she volunteered some information. 'Benjamin's had an accident.'

I choked back a laugh. But if I could keep her talking, stop her hurting me. 'What happened?'

'Was his own fault. If he'd listened to me he'd be all right. So stupid. Some things are meant to be. He knew that – me and Benjamin, nothing could keep us apart – but he tried to leave. How could he do that!' She shrieked and flung the hammer. It hit a row of CDs which clattered to the floor. I saw Benjamin jerk at the noise.

She crossed the room, her feet cracking the CD cases and retrieved the hammer. I sucked in air, my brain febrile with fear, thoughts and pleas bursting like shells on a battlefield.

She sat beside Benjamin on the sofa, the hammer on her lap. I couldn't see any movement from him, no rise and fall of his chest or pulsing in his neck. She drew his hair out of his eyes. Blood fringed his forehead. She took one of his hands and pressed it between her own. 'Why did you spoil it?' she chided him. 'He's always been trouble.' She gave an amused laugh.

'Call an ambulance,' I said.

'Shut up! I couldn't let him leave me. We're engaged.' She held out her hand, tilted it, admiring her ring, her head cocked to one side. 'He's staying here with me. I'm looking after him now.'

My ears were singing as if there was a car alarm going off inside my head but I still registered a noise outside. A vehicle slowing and stopping. Next thing there was knocking at the door, the bell ringing and a loud voice.

'Police! Open the door. Can you hear me? Police!'

Lucy looked bemused. Her eyes darted one way then another. She grabbed the hammer and stood up. Started towards me. I flinched. There is no way to protect your head when your hands are tied behind your back.

'You stupid cow,' she spat at me. 'You've ruined it all.'

'Police! Open the door. Does anyone need

medical attention? We have a doctor here.'

'I've got a doctor,' she said quietly. I doubted the man at the door could hear.

'Help,' I shouted out. 'He needs an ambulance. Get us out of here.'

She kicked me again in the back. It hurt. I wanted to thrash out, rain blows on her, smash that elegant face to putty. I squeezed my eyes tight to stop the tears. I needed to be strong. Use the anger not the fear.

'No,' she shouted, her voice hard. 'Go away!'

She ran from the room and her footsteps vibrated through the house as she went upstairs. I felt her crossing the room above. To look out, I imagined. At the police cordons, the ambulances standing by, the knots of alarmed neighbours and passers-by. Drawn by the spectacle, appalled at the potential for bad news. She'd love it.

'Benjamin,' I gave a loud whisper, 'can you hear me?'

Nothing. I'd read somewhere, talking to someone, or touching them could help them survive a trauma even when they were unconscious.

'The police are here, they'll get us out. We'll get you to hospital. It's going to be all right.'

Inside panic skittered through me. The longer they left us with her the worse our chances were. She seemed oblivious as to whether Benjamin was dead or alive. Another fit of rage and she would turn on me again.

Lucy hurried downstairs and into the lounge.

Help, I thought, please help us now. Help!

'You bitch,' she screamed. 'Why couldn't you leave us alone?' She raised the hammer.

'No!' My teeth gritted together. Maddie, please. Terror burst through my veins.

There was a horrendous crashing sound and I heard Lucy yelp. The room filled with hissing, loud and sibilant. My eyes were burning, awful, like acid on my pupils, hot tears streaming from them but no respite. Smoke choking me. Impossible to see. No breath! I began retching, each spasm inflaming the throbbing pains where she had hammered my shoulder and head and kicked me.

There was clamour and commotion, voices shouting, bulky bodies surging about then hands on my legs, pulling me, dragging me, through glass and splintered wood. Out. Out into the, fresh, cloudy, bloody beautiful daylight.

Chapter Twenty-Five

I couldn't breathe, as if my throat had closed up. My nose was on fire and I could taste the bitter, chemical stench of toxins. My body was jerking in panic then someone clamped a mask to my face and I sucked in air like a swimmer surfacing from a dive. The world kept tilting and it reminded me of the giddying sensation of the minor earthquakes Manchester had experienced. The disconcerting physical feeling that nothing was solid anymore and the peculiar way the tremors travelled through the body, currents through water, a reminder of how much of us is liquid.

Sometime later they took the mask away. A paramedic was releasing my arms. When he finally got them free blades of pain shot through my hands and travelled up my arms. So bad it made me weep. He murmured reassurance and then began to untie my feet.

'We need to see to them cuts.'

I twisted my head to see what he was on about. My trousers had ridden up and there were long slashes on my calves and ankles and ragged tears where the flesh was frilled and bloody from my kicking at the French windows. I couldn't feel anything in my legs. Blood ran freely from one cut and he stuck a big dressing over it.

'Any pain?'

Where did I start? I wiped at my tears and set off the throbbing in my skull.

'My head, shoulder.' Talking made me cough.

'Any double vision?'

'Dizzy.'

'Nasty lump, probably need an x-ray, check for fractures and a stitch or two. What did she hit you with?'

'Hammer.'

'Any nausea?'

Surely he could smell it. 'I was sick.'

'Before the tear gas?'

There was a burst of shouting from inside. I thought I heard Lucy's voice in the midst of it. Then it went quiet. Even though it was cloudy the sky was too bright. I saw a seagull, way up high, storms at sea. Fly away. Stars peppered the fringes of my vision. I closed my eyes.

'How did you know – who rang the police?'

'The hospital – she rang them pretending to be a police officer so she could get his address. They thought it was a bit odd so they checked and we'd a report from the neighbours – windows breaking. That'd be you, would it? Nearly done and then we'll get you to hospital.'

'My little girl.' I opened my eyes and the world slanted. 'Will you ring them? I want to go home.'

He smiled. What a lovely man, I thought. Gratitude swelled in my chest. I wanted to thank him. I tried to open my mouth but everything went soft and swallowed me.

I don't recall being in the ambulance. I woke up on a trolley covered in a blanket under ghastly bright strip lights. My mouth was parched. I narrowed my eyes and looked about but I couldn't see anyone or any way of getting a drink. I fell asleep and was immediately woken by a nurse. When I asked for a drink she explained I couldn't have anything in case I needed a general anaesthetic – an empty stomach was essential.

'How do you know I didn't have a four course meal before I got here?'

'Did you?'

I frowned.

'A doctor will be with you soon.'

Next time I opened my eyes I saw Ray. He looked so serious it frightened me.

'Hello,' I managed.

'Christ!' he said.

I blinked. 'It's not that bad.'

He made a funny noise. 'Oh, Sal!' There was such a depth of emotion in his voice: love and sadness and a profound, unashamed longing in his eyes. I couldn't bear it. I closed my eyes, bit my teeth together and fresh pain flowered through my temples.

'Maddie?' I said eventually.

'Fine. With Sheila.'

'I want to go home.'

'What does the doctor say?'

'I haven't seen one yet.'

He sighed and went in search of someone.

I had to be examined then they wheeled me to x-ray where they took pictures of my head, my shoulder and ribs. A nurse who smelt like an ashtray cleaned and stitched the cuts on my legs and one on my head. I hadn't much room to talk; I smelt pretty foul myself.

They finally let me have a small plastic cup of lukewarm water that tasted of bleach and felt like nectar. Ray waited with me and as the time dragged on there were flashes of normality, of the mundane, in our conversation that I was thankful for.

A policeman, a detective, arrived. Reeking of aftershave and whisky. He asked me about the events leading up to the siege. I gave him a brief outline which was all he wanted at that stage.

'How's Doctor Vernay?'

'I'm afraid he died.'

Oh no, please no. My stomach fell.

'The paramedics tried to revive him but–'

Fear and grief rose in my throat, flapping like birds of ill-omen. I'd led her there, taken her straight to him.

'What about Lucy Barker?'

'She's been charged with his murder.'

Guilt circled me like a stalking horse. The words *what have I done* echoed endlessly.

Chapter Twenty-Six

Doctor Vernay's murder was front page news. Inside features were dedicated to cataloguing the escalating violence that Lucy Barker had subjected him to. Editorials called for increased powers to identify and incarcerate potential killers like Lucy Barker while others argued the case for retaining civil liberties in a world where such murders were statistically very rare. My name was splashed across the pages too; my part described as the stooge, the unwitting private investigator, the hostage who had alerted the police, the dupe.

And of course there were pictures of Benjamin. As best man at a friend's wedding, as a boy on the beach in a rubber dinghy, at his graduation ceremony. Smiling, always smiling.

I managed to function well enough for Maddie and Tom. The saturation coverage meant I couldn't invent a story for my injuries but I underplayed the whole thing, and breathed a sigh of relief when a scandal about a government minister accused of rape pushed the story off the news.

In the days that followed I was tormented. I'd made a living as a private eye for several years. I'd imagined I was good at it. People often came to me because I was recommended. My work was about helping people, about uncovering secrets and lies and finding the truth. Sometimes it was hard to hear and people struggled to cope with what they learnt. My work for Lucy

Barker had cost Benjamin Vernay his life. Blood on my hands.

The police conducted a long series of interviews with me, gathering then checking and re-checking my statements about the events. What Lucy had said when, her behaviour, what I had heard and seen at the doctor's house. They were very thorough but considerate, stopping whenever I needed a break or became distressed.

I picked over my dealings with Lucy. Surely a decent detective would have known Lucy Barker was bad news? I'd found her cold and awkward and I'd blamed that for my uneasy feelings about her. At some deeper level I must have known she was dangerous. Once I knew she'd lied to me I should have dropped the case. Why hadn't I spotted her mendacity, her scheming? I'd danced to her sick tune like a puppet.

She's very plausible. He'd said that. But it didn't help. I questioned whether I was good enough to do the job any more. I was heartsick, disillusioned and aching with regret. I had no peace.

If I folded up the business what could I do? With no marketable skills I could find work in a call centre or as a cashier. Or stay home with the children and take up Ray's offer of paying for Tom's care.

I tried to recall the cases I'd investigated that had worked out well. Families reunited, vulnerable people protected from conmen, fraudsters unmasked, criminals brought to justice. And the people who, at the end of their tether, had screwed up their courage, scraped together money and come to me: Agnes Donlan worried about her old friend Lily, Janice Hobbs desperate to find her missing son, Jimmy Achebe fearful that his wife was cheating on him, Luke Wallace, a terrified teenager locked up and charged with killing his best mate. Faces and voices came back to me, words of gratitude, letters of heartfelt thanks. Worse moments when I'd had to deliver terrible news and seen people's hopes strangled and their lives turned upside down. The times I had sat with someone while they tried to swallow the bitter truth.

I didn't know if I could do that again. Without me Benjamin Vernay would still have been alive.

So wrong. How could I have been so appallingly wrong?

One weekend evening I was in the garden.

287

May had arrived and I was planting up pots with pansies, petunia, lobelia and alyssum plugs, white geraniums and nasturtium seeds. I'd plenty of ivy and baby conifers left from the winter boxes that I could re-use and some fuchsias that looked like dead sticks but would flourish come the summer. The light was fading but the pansies seemed bright against the gloom. Maddie and Tom, staying up late, had discovered some chalk and drawn a target on the back wall. They were lobbing 'arrows' made of pea sticks at it.

'We need a bow,' said Tom

'Two bows,' said Maddie.

'I don't think we've anything bendy enough to make a bow,' I told them. Ray knocked on the window and held his hand to his ear, little finger and thumb making a phone shape.

'Hello,' the woman said when I answered. 'I got your name from a friend Chris – in Hebden Bridge?'

'Oh, yes.'

'She said you run a detective agency. You see I'm worried about my partner – she's missing and–'

Caroline! Shock flashed through my arms, my skin tightened and anger rose in my throat. Of all the bloody nerve.

'You beat her up,' I said baldly. 'If she had any sense she'd prosecute. Don't ever call here again.' I replaced the phone, shaking and stunned at the gall of the woman.

Diane took me out for a meal. Minty was still at hers, she was paying rent and would sort something else out by the end of the month. Diane filled the silence with talk about her work, she hadn't got the residency at the infirmary but there was a chance of part-time lecturing at the university. It would mean regular income but she was worried it would squeeze out the time she had to work on her own pieces. We were half way through the main course when Diane finally got round to asking me 'So, what's next?'

Suddenly I was full. I stirred the sliced potato around in the mushroom and brandy jus and tried to frame a reply. 'Don't know. Wait and see.' I couldn't meet her gaze. 'You could try the lecturing for a year,' I tried to divert her, 'see how it goes.'

'It wasn't your fault,' she said.

'I took her straight to him.'

'No,' she reached across and grabbed my arm, looking at me keenly. Her grip insisting

I make eye contact. 'She would have found him sooner or later.'

'I should have followed my instincts. I didn't trust her but I kept on working for her.'

'You didn't know she was a psychopath. She fooled everyone.'

'He's dead, Diane.'

'She'd have killed eventually. That's what they're saying.'

I was shaking my head.

'You can't keep blaming yourself. Look at you.'

I pushed away from the table, began to rise, aware of the stares from other diners.

'And it's bloody self-indulgent.'

I gawped at her, felt heat flare in my cheeks. The nerve! Shoving the chair back I went off to the toilets. She followed me, shutting the door from the stairs behind her.

'You didn't hold the hammer. You didn't kill him. Wallowing in it won't help anyone.'

Furious I rounded on her. 'For Christ sake, this isn't some little upset. The man is dead.'

'Yes,' her eyes flashed. 'But it's not your fault. Lucy Barker killed him and she's in Broadmoor. Locked away so she can't do it again. He's dead but you're not. You've got a life. Get on with it.'

I glared at her, wanting to thump her and felt even angrier because I knew there was truth in what she said.

She held up her palms. 'Lecture over. Are you going to have a sweet? I think I deserve one after that little lot.'

I tried to smile. 'You go down.'

My face in the mirror was miserable, my eyes had a brittle, wounded look. Ghastly. Diane was right logically but there was a gulf between that and the emotions overwhelming me. Even if I held onto the thought that Lucy Barker may have killed without my involvement there was another sentiment eating away at me. He was dead and I wasn't. My escape made me feel very, very lucky and sick with guilt.

Ray had been very busy since my return. I began to think it had all blown over until one afternoon when he came in with a bag over his shoulder. He bent to fuss Digger. I was at the kitchen table staring at a cookery book trying to find something new to make that wouldn't take a week to prepare and involve ingredients I'd have to go to use my investigative skills to hunt down.

Ray looked at me, his eyes friendly. 'The

bruising has almost gone.'

I nodded. On the outside.

He straightened up. Slid his bag onto a chair.

'Laura and me,' he said.

My neck prickled, my heart squeezed tight, I braced myself. Marriage? A baby? Moving?

'We've finished.'

I gawped at him. 'But why?'

He regarded me steadily. His eyes brown and clear.

I looked away.

'Sal.'

'No. I can't do this.'

He put his hand out and covered mine, the skin on his fingers slightly rough against my knuckles. 'Tell me you don't feel it, too,' he whispered. I could see the tracery of lines beside his eyes, dark eyes smouldering. I felt my pulse accelerate, a physical craving betray me.

'No,' I whispered back, my lips felt swollen, my breath stuttered.

'Liar,' he said and his lips touched mine, soft and dry, fringed by the springy hair of his moustache. I closed my eyes. Dizzy, I wanted to give in, to dissolve. A tremor rippled through me. He kissed me. In my head voices: no don't, stop, oh, don't stop, yes, oh yes.

The shrill of the doorbell jerked us apart. I stood quickly feeling shameful and confused and giddy.

'Sal,' he blurted out urgently. He wanted an answer but it was too big for me to handle. All too much.

I shook my head, covered my mouth with my hand.

I looked at him. His face pale with emotion, his eyes glittering.

'I don't know,' I said. And walked away to answer the door.

Chapter Twenty-Seven

First thing the next day I forced myself round to the office to collect the mail and messages. It was warm outside, hard now to take in how recently frost had scoured the land.

I let myself in and picked up the pile of letters and flyers for me on the hallstand. I made my way downstairs, unlocked the door and went in. A fine layer of dust covered everything. My cactus looked okay – that's why I'd bought it. The mail included payment from a former client and a handwritten note.

Thank you so much for all your help. Nick is in Rehab and we hope he'll stick with it though it's early days. Without you we would never have got this far. Best wishes, Charlie and Monica.

I was moved. The family had been to hell and back with their son and his drug addiction.

But I couldn't face it any more. Too many sad stories. I'd had enough of the tragedies and deceit and suspicion.

And I had failed.

I had started seeing a counsellor; someone I could pore over the memories with and pick at the shame and the blame. She was a good listener. Like Diane, she thought I was being too hard on myself. She reminded me of how I had tried to save Benjamin Vernay, she pointed out that I had not held the hammer. I heard what she was saying but it didn't help the feelings. It would be a long time before I made my peace.

The file with the details of Lucy's case was on my desk. I let it lie there. I didn't know what else to do. Ray had always hated the jeopardy my work could throw at me. He'd be relieved to see me in a safer occupation. But this wasn't about him. I didn't want to think about him. Another part of my future undecided. So much in flux. I heard the bell ring, climbed the steps to answer it.

Minty was on the doorstep.

'I called at the house. Ray said you were here. Are you okay? If it's not a good time... I just wanted to thank you.'

I nodded. 'I'm fine.' Invited her in, made a drink.

She looked much better, the bruises had faded, she'd had her hair trimmed and the clothes she wore looked new.

I deflected her questions about work. 'Heavy stuff, I'm still dealing with it. What about you?'

'Fine.' It sounded brittle and we both heard it. 'Well,' she amended, 'one day at a time.' She clasped her cup, head dipped she looked up at me. 'I still love her. Can you believe that. It's stupid. I think about her all the time – about it being different...'

She saw I was about to speak.

'I know it can't be,' she hurried on, 'I won't go back. I'm moving actually. Milton Keynes,' she rolled her eyes. 'With the cows.'

I smiled.

'I know a couple of people there. Don't know whether I'm running away.'

'No. It's a brave move, braver than staying.'

'The devil you know and all that?'

'Yes.'

'So I wanted to thank you.'

'I didn't...'

'If you hadn't stopped, if I hadn't met you,' she shook her head. 'When you gave me your card,' she laughed, 'a private eye. Just seemed like it was fate. Someone telling me something. A way out. Do you know what I mean?'

'I'm not sure.'

'Like you were meant to find me and once you had there was someone I could turn to.'

'It was Diane that put you up,' I shrugged.

'She was great. And the food – she should open a restaurant.'

She didn't stay much longer and we made small talk for the rest of her visit. Seeing her out I wished her luck.

'And you. Thanks again,' her voice trembled and I sensed her emotion. She gave me a clumsy hug and hurried off. My eyes filled with tears, everything seemed to set me off. Like a valve had gone.

I re-recorded the message on my answer phone. *You've reached Sal Kilkenny investigations. This office is not currently taking on any new clients.*

It would give me breathing space until I finally made up my mind.

When I checked it back it sounded very muffled. I disconnected the machine and ejected the tape, blew the fluff out of the inside.

While I was doing that the phone rang. Sounded like a young man. He spoke in a very stilted way, his voice shook and I realised that he was reading his lines out loud. He'd written down what he wanted to say.

'I got your name from the Yellow Pages. I wonder if you can help me. I was adopted in Manchester in nineteen seventy-five and I want to try and find my birth mother.'

'I'm sorry,' I began.

'Don't you do that?' He blurted out. 'Only it said in the book...'

There was a pause.

'You do find people, don't you?'

I hesitated.

'Please,' he said. 'It's not something I'm doing on the spur of the moment. It's not been easy. I just ... I've thought about it such a lot, you don't know ... Please, if you–'

'I don't–' I faltered.

'Are you all right?'

That simple question, his concern for me even though he was wracked with nerves. That did it.

'Yes.'

I sat down, took a breath and picked up a pen.

The publishers hope that this book has given you enjoyable reading. Large Print Books are especially designed to be as easy to see and hold as possible. If you wish a complete list of our books please ask at your local library or write directly to:

Magna Large Print Books
Magna House, Long Preston,
Skipton, North Yorkshire.
BD23 4ND

This Large Print Book, for people
who cannot read normal print,
is published under the auspices of

THE ULVERSCROFT FOUNDATION

... we hope you have enjoyed this book.
Please think for a moment about those
who have worse eyesight than you ...
and are unable to even read or enjoy
Large Print without great difficulty.

You can help them by sending a
donation, large or small, to:

**The Ulverscroft Foundation,
1, The Green, Bradgate Road,
Anstey, Leicestershire, LE7 7FU,
England.**
or request a copy of our brochure for
more details.

The Foundation will use all donations
to assist those people who are visually
impaired and need special attention
with medical research, diagnosis
and treatment.

Thank you very much for your help.

Other MAGNA Titles
In Large Print

ANNE BAKER
Merseyside Girls

JESSICA BLAIR
The Long Way Home

W. J. BURLEY
The House Of Care

MEG HUTCHINSON
No Place For A Woman

JOAN JONKER
Many A Tear Has To Fall

LYNDA PAGE
All Or Nothing

NICHOLAS RHEA
Constable Over The Bridge

MARGARET THORNTON
Beyond The Sunset